Emily and the Gnomes

The World of Valencia

By

S.D. Michaels

For my sister Karen and those like her, who work every day educating people on the plight of our world's marine life.

The World of Valencia

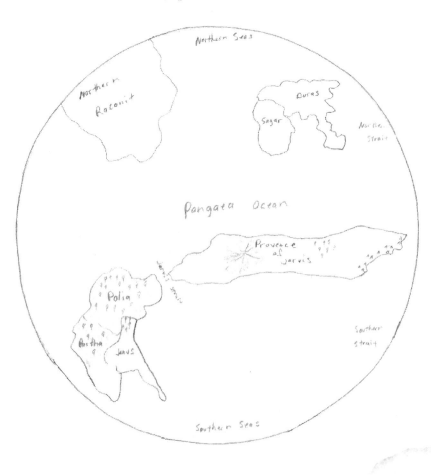

The World of Valencia

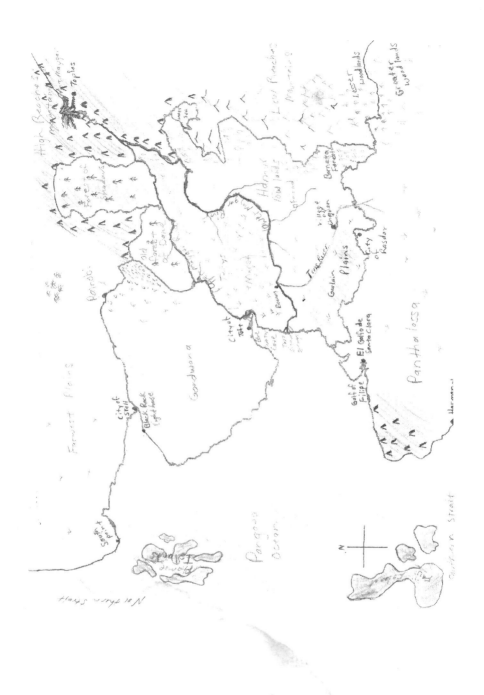

5

Chapter One

Jabaz: father of all the gods, creator of all the heavens and the cosmos, journeyed through the glimmering lights of his universe. With purpose, he traveled past all the planets, moons and stars until he came to a spot that suited his need, and below him he created a sphere, at first a formless and darkened void. After a moment of thought, he placed land and water on the globe and hovered over his creation pondering his next move.

With a single thought, a golden ball of fire appeared above him, shining light down onto his world. This is good, he thought to himself, but I mustn't forget, there needs to be night as well as day. He separated the light from the darkness and set the sphere into a slow spin.

He'd done this so many times before, making each of his worlds a little different from the others. But this one, this one was for Ava, the youngest of his daughters, the most ambitious, and for the time being, his favorite.

"She wants plants," he said, waving a hand and covering the planet with various types of foliaged, trees, bushes, ground cover, and even plants to live in the water. "And seas teeming with living creatures, and birds to fill the sky. And let there be beasts to live and roam the lands," he said, glancing beside him at his daughter. "And let there be no humans to bring them harm, but little Gnomes to guard and care for my creation."

Ava smiled and kissed her father's cheek. "Perfect," she said, with excitement. "It's just like Emily's world of Valencia. Well, kind of."

Jabaz shook his head, not understanding his daughter's fascination with a human's prayers she once heard from a forgotten world he had created and abandoned a long, long, time ago. "You know the rules," he said, as his form started to fade. "Terra is yours, treat it well."

Emily climbed out of her old beat up Chevy truck and walked around to the back to grab her gear. Today's rescue was a little different from ones in the past where they were saving injured animals who had been cut up by the propellers of passing speed boats. Today they had five presumably healthy manatees stuck in a small pond on the outskirts of a shopping mall. The call came in early in morning from a concerned citizen who spotted the trapped animals while walking her dog around the mall's perimeter. Best guess was that a strong storm surge was caused by the Category 3 hurricane that had hit the area over the weekend, allowing the manatees to swim from a nearby river into the pond where they were then stranded after the water level returned to normal.

Tugging on a wetsuit, Emily listened to the others who had come out to help with the rescue. She herself had degrees in Marine Science and Biology, and had gotten her Master's from the University of Stell. She had been on hundreds of animal rescues after her move to Toft from Stell six years ago and landed a job at the Upper Maygar River Rescue and Rehab Center. Paul and Tiffany from Toft Fish and Wildlife were also there, along with Toft Aquarium and Animal Rescue team Matt, Brian, and

Ashley. The plan, she was told, was to herd the animals into the shallow end of the pond where they could be netted and removed safely from the water.

It's funny, though, that even with all the best laid plans, the animals that are being rescued never seem to get the message of how the whole rescue scenario is supposed to play out. After an hour of chasing, splashing, dunking, and other such excitements, a ten foot, 1,200 pound lactating female was hoisted out of the water by a small crane onto the back of a flatbed truck, and hauled into the processing tent. Soon afterwards, her baby was corralled and brought up to join her, followed by the remaining three animals in twenty to thirty minute intervals. A team of veterinarians and their assistants from the university took the standard blood, urine and fecal samples from each of the animals, which were all deemed healthy and loaded onto the transport trucks to be taken and released back into the watery inlet about a mile away.

Leaving the rest of the team to clean up and finalize all the paperwork with the mall, city and state, Emily returned to her truck. After toweling off her hands and face, she checked her cell phone for messages. There were several, but she skipped to the one sent by Deb, a friend that she had grown up and gone to college with, and who was still living in the Stell area. Deb had sent her a news link from the Northern Straits Orca research center where they had both worked while in school. An adult female whale, approximately 24 feet in length, was found floating in the water near the Southwestern tip of the Farwest Plains, emaciated, but with no other signs of trauma.

Emily dialed her friend. "What the heck, Deb," she said, unzipping her suit. "That makes five in the past two years.

And this one's only a couple of weeks after that calf was found off Black Rock Point."

"I know it's really sad about that calf. DNA shows that it was from NS20's group, a little girl born sometime in early spring. But as far as the adults, there's only been one other confirmed death, NS44. The others are still labeled as missing."

"They're dead, we both know it."

"I know."

"It's obviously the food shortage."

"I know."

"The salmon runs, they're getting worse every year."

"I know."

"The whales don't have enough to eat!"

"I know."

"They are literally starving to death."

"I know."

"All right, since you know everything then tell me this, when will it be too late to do something about it?"

Deb heaved a heavy sigh. "That, I don't know. I'm sorry Em, I knew the news would upset you, I wasn't sure I should even send it to you. You have so much to worry about down where you are now. You still working with the manatees in Blue Water Cove?"

"Yeah, I helped start a petition asking the Valencia Fish and Wildlife Service to make the Two Sister Springs a winter sanctuary for them. The poor things, every time they arrive there they get accosted by thousands of people who either deny them access to or chase them from the warm-water cove."

"I hear you. Remember when you left, there were maybe a half dozen boats tracking the pods up here?"

"Yeah…"

"Well it's quadruple that now. Besides the government boats chasing them around, we've had a couple dozen whale watching groups that popped up. The poor whales don't get a moment's peace. No matter where they go someone always spots them, from land, boat, or air, then radios their location to the others and the circus starts all over again."

Emily exhaled and leaned back against the side of her truck. "I wish we could just send them all away, to a place where they would be safe from all mankind."

"I know. Me too."

Chapter Two

Hidden in the vegetation and underbrush beside the water's edge, six little Gnomes gathered around the pond. The spectacle of the humans in the water was enjoyable to watch, but they had a job to do. The Wise One spotted the human they were to help, and signaled the others to follow her as she moved away from the water.

Ava had given them no instructions other than to, 'help the one named Emily save her animals, and do not let the other humans see you.' Without the ability to use or understand magic, spotting a Gnomes would confuse or scare the poor human and Ava didn't want to chance that. To help in their quest, their goddess had given the Gnomes the ability to communicate with both the humans and the creatures of this world. But as for how they were to move them to their world, they had only a glimpse of an idea.

Waiting in the shadows, the Gnomes listened as the human named Emily spoke. 'I wish we could just send them all away, to a place where they would be safe from all mankind.'

The youngest of the group started jumping around by the human's feet trying to get her attention. "That's why we're here," he shouted. "We came to help you."

"It's neither the right time nor the right place for introduction," said The Wise One, pulling the youngster back under the object the human was leaning against. "There are too many of her kind around, and we must not be seen."

"Wise One," The Little Female said. "She came here in this thing, it would be logical to believe that she'll use it to leave the area as well."

The Wise One nodded. "I believe you're right."

"She left that part opened after pulling out her extra skin."

The Wise One nodded again. "Obviously needed for entering the water," he said. "Interesting, I will have to get a better look at it when the opportunity arises. Quickly now, let us move inside and keep out of sight."

The Gnomes scurried up the back of the truck and ducked under and around the tools and trash that littered the truck bed.

The Wise One was just starting to settle into a dark cave that smelled like a variety of different animals when he heard a startling cry from outside.

Peeking out, he spotted The Little Female staring straight ahead. "He went inside," she said, pointing at the closed off area. "The Young One, he went inside where the human sits."

Suddenly, with no warning, they were blanketed with a wet dark object. The Wise One pulled The Little Female into the stinky cave and moved to the back where they could escape the dampness. "Most unfortunate," The Wise One said. "I have no idea where the rest of our group is, and I believe," he said, bracing against the walls of the cave. "This thing is moving."

On her days off, if she wasn't at the library giving lectures on the plight of the endangered animals of their world, Emily could be found down at the beach. Gondwana's coast line is known for its beautiful sandy beaches, and boasts a wide array of scenic parks for picnicking, camping, and hiking, and there were plenty of grassy areas where you could throw down a blanket and whittle away the day just staring up at the clouds. There are over 20 parks along the Gondwana southwestern coastline alone. This is where Emily did some of her best work, whether it was being under a covered pavilion talking with old people lounging in their chairs, or out in the sun down by the crashing waves with a bunch of kids, teaching them about conservation and preservation. She was a firm believer in the old saying that 'children are our future', and she worked tirelessly at educating whomever she could on the struggles of their world's endangered animals.

So after spending the morning wrangling manatees, she headed for her other hot spot among the surf and the sand and found a group of young students who had volunteered to pick up trash on the beach. She approached the group and spoke with the adults in charge. She was in luck, they were just about ready to take a break and let the kids have a rest. Emily moved to front of the group and introduced herself.

"Hello, my name is Emily Dickens, and I understand that you're from West Town Elementary?"

A roar came up from the children.

Emily smiled and nodded. "Let me tell you a little bit about myself. I'm a Biologist from the University of Toft, and I work as a conservationist. Can anyone tell me what a conservationist does?"

Emily heard a lot of mumbling but none of the kids could answer her question. Finally she answered it for them. "A conservationist is a person who advocates, or acts, for the protection and preservation of the environment and wildlife. I know," she said, hearing a couple of grumbles coming from the group. "It's a lot of big words, but what it means is that I work to protect the animals and forests of our world from being lost forever."

There was a lot of giggling and comments about lost and found posters. But Emily stayed on track and jumped into her spiel. "I have a question for all of you. Can anyone one tell me what the number one killer in the world's oceans is?" She asked, looking out over the crowd of about thirty people.

"Sharks!" shouted a boy in the back.

"Yeah, Great Whites," another boy said. "They're huge."

"Barracudas," someone else shouted out. "I saw something on T.V. about barracudas killing things."

"Jellyfish," a small timid girl said from the front. "They almost killed Dory and Marlin."

"Killer Whales," yelled another girl in front of Emily. "They're the biggest."

Emily knelt in front of the boisterous girl. "No, it's not a Killer Whale, it's actually, man!" she said firmly. Rising to her feet, she repeated the correct answer to the crowd. "Man is the number one killer in our world's oceans. In truth, he's the number one killer in the whole world, but let's stick to the water right now."

Emily started to pace as she spoke to the gathering of people. "It's estimated that over 1 million seabirds, and 100,000 sea mammals are killed by pollution every year. Can you kids give me some names of sea mammals?"

"Killer Whales," the girl in front said loudly.

Emily smiled, "Yes, Killer Whales. What else?"

"Seals," someone shouted.

"Yes, and?"

"Bigger whales?" a boy on her right said.

"Yes," Emily laughed, "Can you think of anything else?"

There was silence for a moment, then Emily said, "There was a movie out not long ago, does anyone remember what kind of animal Winter was?"

"A Dolphin," everyone shouted.

"Yes," she laughed. "A Dolphin. Dolphins, porpoises, whales, seals, manatees, sea otters, walruses, seals, sea-lions, they are all sea mammals, and over a 100,000 of these beautiful creatures are killed every year by pollution."

Emily asked an adult for some of the trash the kids had picked up off the beach. Picking out a few items she held them up and said, "Stuff like plastic bags, foam rubber, and other items deadly to sea life and dumped into the ocean are sometime eaten by marine mammals, fish, and birds that mistake it for food." Emily put the trash back in the bag and picked up something else that the group had found on the beach. "Discarded fishing nets drift for years, ensnaring fish and mammals," she said, holding up the piece of net. "In certain regions, ocean currents corral trillions of decomposing plastic items and other trash into gigantic, swirling garbage patches. One in the Northern Seas, known as the Northern Trash Vortex, is estimated to be the size of the Mount Maygar, and on top of that, a new massive patch was discovered in the Southern Seas just a couple of years ago. But the biggest killer by far is the introduction of toxins into the animal's environment – it has affected every square mile of ocean on this planet and impacted about 40 percent of ocean's ecosystem.

"The Orcas, or Killer Whales as you called them," she said, resting a hand on the little girl's shoulder, "are just one of ten marine animals that have been found to hold toxins from their environment in their blubber. In other words, when men over-fish in the areas where orcas live and there's not enough fish for them to eat, they often die when relying on their body fat or blubber to sustain them. Or if they're young and don't have toxins build up in their fat yet, they just simply starve to death."

"What about Iceberg?" a woman standing outside the group of children yelled.

Emily steadied herself for the confrontation. "For those of you who don't know, Iceberg is an albino, or an all-white adult orca who's believed to be around 45 year of age, who was captured along with seven other orcas from his family group in the early 1970's from the Northern Straits. All the other whales have since perished."

The woman moved up closer to the front and met Emily's gaze. The lady's eyes reflected her dislike for Emily's presence. "Do you think it is right for that rare albino or any of the other whales, for that matter, to be kept in fish bowls?"

"No, but tell me truthfully, have you ever been to the Stell Marine Park and seen Iceberg?" Before the woman could answer Emily turned to the others." How many here have been to the Stell Marine Park, or for that matter any another kind of aquarium or marine park?"

The response from the crowd was a positive and resounding yes. Facing the woman again she added. "The animals in aquariums, sea parks, and zoos are there for educational purposes. People learn from them."

"That's not true," the woman spat. "We use them for entertainment. We have them put on shows for their food. They should all be let go."

"Where to?" Emily asked, sweeping her arm to the water. "Into the world's polluted, and over-fished oceans to die along with their cousins?"

"Better to die free than to live in a cage."

"I'm sorry, but I don't agree," Emily said calmly but firmly. She moved to within a couple of feet of the woman it was time for her to be the forceful one. "How can you be so selfish? What was once good enough for all of us is now some kind of stigma for you. Those whales in their fish bowls, as you call them, may be the only Orcas around for our children or children's children to see. I encourage you to leave the ones in the aquariums alone and put your

resources and efforts into saving those animals in the wild

which we are slowly, but surely, **eradicating!**

Chapter Three

The midday sun soon became too much for the small group of Gnomes to handle. Moving from the back of the truck into the shade, they stood for a moment looking out from under Emily's transportation device, watching the antics of the youngest Gnome as he scurried across the beach.

"Hot, hot, very hot," the youngster exclaimed as he danced over the sand. "Oh, my, oh my poor feet. Hot, hot, very hot."

The Wise One pulled the jumping Gnome into the shade and sat him down by the oldest of their kind. "Where have you been?" The Wise One asked. "And where is Emily?"

"Back there," he said, rubbing his feet. "She's back there talking to the small ones. I was watching from her pouch."

"Pouch?" the tallest Gnome asked with bewilderment. "I didn't know humans had pouches."

"Not that kind of a pouch," the youngest said, standing up. "This one is removable, I climbed into it when I entered the seating area."

The Large Female Gnome on his right wiped a brown substance off his chin. "What is this?" she asked, examining the smooth material on her fingers.

The youngest bit his lip and kicked at the ground with the toe of his leather boot. "Well," he mumbled. "There's a lot of it, and I didn't consume much."

"Explain?" The Wise One said sternly.

"They're in the pouch, long thin blocks of them. They smelled delicious. The wrapping was open on one, so I took a bite. Well, maybe two bites."

The Large Female warily tasted the stuff on her fingers. "It's very good," she exclaimed, licking her hand clean. "Can I have some more?"

"I want some," the Tall Gnome huffed. "When the human returns, I'll ride in her pouch."

"No, that's my spot," the youngest squeaked.

The Wise One moved away from the two who were bickering onto the edge of the sand, and as he looked out across the beach he spotted Emily coming back their way. "This discussion is over," he said, interrupting them. "She's returning and we all need to hide." Grabbing the collar of the youngest one's shirt, he added, "You're riding with me in the cave."

31

Emily hopped into her truck and pulled out her phone before starting the engine. A message popped up on the screen. Stell Marine Park was celebrating another dolphin birth. She scrolled down to read some of the comments.

Sarah Martin: These animals need to be put back in the wild.

Piper Willing: really? They are at a place where everything is done for them to thrive. Even a poor child born in a bad section of town gets less care than this dolphin will. Sure, release them into the ocean where they have no chance at survival thanks to man. This isn't fantasy land lady, it's the real world. I know we've all seen the videos of dolphin and other sea mammals swimming and leaping and think all is going wonderfully, same as seeing people enjoying a day in the sun, but that doesn't mean the struggle is over. Their environment is contaminated and mankind is overfishing their oceans. If the pollution, doesn't get them, starvation will, but sure, keep thinking your lie of it being so much better out there.

Emily chuckled, she knew Piper from other rescues she'd been on. For twenty years he had worked with dolphins at the marine park and he loved to educate people when it came to his precious pets.

Emily read on.

Sarah Martin: NO, NO, NO.....!! Take them back to the ocean where they belong.....

Paul Hackler: The Ocean has been made inhabitable by humans and the dolphins are dying all the time in floating fishing line and nets, also their food supply is being taken away by over fishing, the ocean also has way more ships out there than it used to which interferes with how the dolphins find their food.

Heath Carsic: Sarah you're defiantly uneducated.

Emily was about to put her own two cents into the mix but got distracted by a noise coming from the bed of the truck. Hopping out of the cab she studied her belongings. 2 wet suits, one 6 mil, one 3 mil, a pair of aqua shoes, tanks, snorkel, flippers, buoyancy regulator, tool box, cat carrier. And the bag from yesterday's lunch, torn open. "Probably a gull trying to get to the scraps," she said grabbing the opened bag and carrying it to a nearby trash can. Once done, she went back to the truck, climbed in and started the engine.

"So what's for dinner," she asked herself while backing the truck out of its parking space. "I haven't had a sub in a while, maybe I'll stop and get a Blaze-n-House sub for dinner. Oh yeah, a Pastrami grinder. That'll hit the spot."

The Wise Gnome studied the Tall One for a moment before he spoke. "She almost caught you, what were you thinking?"

"I'm sorry, Wise One. I'm just so hungry."

The Wise One sighed. "Perhaps we'll find nourishment in her shelter."

The six Gnomes looked up at the structure in front of them. Emily had gone through the door and now they were stuck on the other side, wondering how to get in.

"She turned the shiny thing up there," The Tall One said.

"I know that," said The Wise One. "But even if we could reach it, I don't think we would be strong enough to turn it."

"Maybe there's another way in," said the Large Female.

Five Gnomes moved as a group, looking up and down the walls of the structure for a way inside.

The youngest stayed at the front of the closure to ponder for a minute. Sudden a small flap at the bottom of the door pushed forward and a furry grey head peered out at him. "Hello," he said, in a startled voice. "Can I get in that way?"

The furry creature came out and sniffed the Gnome. "You're not a rat," the creature said, rubbing against the little spirit and almost knocking him over. "And you're not a squirrel, and you kind of smell like my human."

"Probably because I was in her pouch today. And please don't do that," he said, pushing the creature away. "Your hair tickles my nose. And can you tell me if Emily is for sure the human we're speaking of?"

"Emily, yes," it purred. "I have heard her called that before. And so what are you called?"

"I am a Gnome, they call me The Young One. And you?"

"A cat, of course. My human calls me Zoe."

"Well Zoe, back to my first question. Can I get in the way you came out?"

"Of course, Young One, the door swings both ways."

"Excellent. Now all I need to do is find the others and show them the door."

"The others?" the cat purred. "Are they Gnomes like you?"

"Yes," the youngest said with excitement. "There are six of us in all."

The cat counted aloud, "one, two, three, four, five, and you make six. That must be them."

The youngest looked behind him at his friends. "Hi there. This is Zoe."

"We heard," the larger female said.

"Well, she's shown me a way inside."

"We heard that as well," The Wise One said, moving up to the flap and pushing it inward. "Would you mind going in first, Zoe, then let us know where your human is now?"

Zoe sighed and moved past the Gnomes to re-enter the house. Popping her head back out she said, "in case you're wondering, this is called a cat door."

Chapter Four

Emily dried her short brown hair with the towel as she walked out of the bathroom and into her bedroom. Lying on the floor in front of her was her backpack with all its contents spilled out onto the carpet. She was cursing her cat for getting up on the bed and knocking it off, until she noticed some of the candy bars that she'd had put in there for a quick snack were torn into, and half eaten. She looked at the tiny teeth marks in the candy then yelled for the cat. "Zoe!"

The cat peeked around the corner, then slowly meandered over to her.

Emily shook the candy bars at her. "Something got into my stuff. You better get busy and chase it out of here."

Zoe purred as she rubbed against Emily's leg.

"Do you understand me?" Emily asked. "This is making you look pretty bad."

Zoe laid down and started grooming her long grey fur at her owner's feet.

"You're useless." Emily tossed the half eaten candy bars into a small trash can in the bathroom and finished getting dressed.

By the time she had gotten home from her day of manatee-wrangling and lecturing at the beach, she'd been feeling pretty grungy, and was glad to get the smell of the pond out of her hair and put some clean clothes on. Grabbing her cell phone off the bed she quickly checked for any new messages. After seeing there were none, she went out into the front room, moved over to her desk, and turned on her computer. At this point she was ravenous, so she unwrapped her sandwich and took a couple of bites while scanning the file she had created for her orca research. Most of the whale's age information she had collected from 3 sources. Northern Straits Orca Network, Valencia's Cetacean Cousins and Gondwana's Cetacean Base. She entered the information she had gotten today on the adult female who was found in the water near the Southwestern tip of the Farwest Plains. The necropsy information she didn't have, but she still had some friends back home in Stell who might be able to help her.

She took a couple more bites out of her sandwich, then scanned the 4 by 6 foot map of the world which hung on her wall in front of her desk, which displayed all the endangered, vulnerable, and threatened animals on earth.

The Black Rhino, endangered. The Garlain Rhino, endangered. The High Reaches Mountain Gorilla, the Eastern Lowland Gorilla, The Farwest Elephant, Rhino, and Orangutan, all endangered. The list was overwhelming and sometimes too much to bear. The Amur Leopard, Maygar River Gorilla, Gulf of Filipe Porpoise, Faiji Island Deer, Harmur Lowlands Pangolin, all on the verge of extinction and considered critically endangered. She studied the map for a moment longer, looking at the animals that hit a little closer to home for her. The manatee, which she had worked with for the last six years, had been switched off the endangered list to vulnerable, but the Northern Straits Orcas who lived in the waters close to where she grew up in Stell were moved to the endangered list, which the activists used when they were pushing to get Iceberg released from captivity.

"Uh," she moaned. That's another really sad story that both her and her friend Deb back in Stell had been personally involved with. But instead of trying to get Iceberg returned to Northern Straits to be reunited with his pod (which they knew would be a reckless, cruel, and disastrous experiment since Iceberg had been in captivity over 40 years at that time), Emily and Deb were realists and pushed to get the Stell Marine Park to expand their Orca pool to 6 million gallons and to make it orca-friendly, with a 60 feet depth and spots where a killer whale could rub and scratch himself. Also part of the plan was to get Iceberg a friend, but of course that just raised even more criticism from those who were working to get all orcas in captivity released back to the wild, whether born there or not. Emily just couldn't understand why some people thought living in a sea pen in polluted water, (because that's how all of the world's oceans and seas were now), was better than having the whales remain in their tanks with clean filtered salt water, ample food, and attention from adoring fans, trainers, and nameless numbers of scientists.

Emily was fuming about the woman on the beach, and was just about ready to give Deb another call when she heard a loud crashing noise come from the bathroom.

Certain that Zoe had gotten into something that she could break, she raced into her bedroom. Emily had to do a quick maneuver of sidesteps and hops to avoid stepping on the animal scurrying toward her. "*What was that?*" she said, jumping onto the bed. Hearing another noise coming from the bathroom, she cursed under her breath. "Great. Whatever that was, there's two of them."

She had worked with some of the most dangerous animals in the world and never broke a sweat, but small fast creatures, like rats, or worse, mice, she hated. "Okay," she said, trying to calm herself. Climbing off the bed, she grabbed one of the heaviest biology books she had off her book shelf, and steeled herself to enter the room. The bathroom was very small, holding only a pedestal sink, toilet, and shower stall. There really wasn't anywhere for a small furry creature to hide. Suddenly she heard the noise again and saw the trash can rock slightly. Holding the book over her head, she approached the can slowly. "It's got to be a mouse, or maybe a rat? That thing that ran out of here was way too big for a mouse, though." Without looking inside, she quickly placed the book over the trash can, trapping whatever it was inside.

Emily nearly leaped out of her skin when her cat Zoe started rubbing against her leg. "Oh, sure, now you want to help."

Emily slowly picked up the trash can with the book on top and headed for the front door. "Why don't you go get the one that ran that way," she yelled at the cat. "You're supposed to be keeping these things out of here. You lazy feline."

Unceremoniously, she tossed the cheap little trash can and her expensive biology book out onto the front lawn. But curiosity got the best of her, so instead of going inside, she simply stepped back about five feet, and waited for whatever was in the trash can to come out. Several minutes passed before the head of the trapped creature peeked around the side. Emily strained her eyes not believing what it was that she saw. It was no mouse, or rat, but a little man with brown hair, wearing a pointy hat, brownish-green trousers and shirt made from felt or something that looked like moss and leaves, a wide belt, and black leather shoes.

In bewilderment, she stood for a long time just staring at the small creature. Thinking out loud she said. "What the heck are you?"

The Young One straightened his hat, brushed himself off and stepped out of the overturned trash can. "Hello Emily."

"Huh?"

"I said hello."

"You know my name?" she stammered.

"Yes, it was told to us by the goddess Ava."

Emily stumbled back and sat down hard on the front door step. "Who?"

"Ava, she's the goddess of our world."

Emily was starting to think that maybe she'd spent too much time out in the sun today and was starting to hallucinate. "Right," she said, slowly rising to her feet. Turning, she quickly jumped into the house and slammed the door. But that didn't solve her problem. Because standing in the middle of her front room were five other little people.

"Hello Emily. They call me The Wise One. Perhaps you should sit while we talk."

Like the one outside, these little people were wearing pointy hats and some kind of clothing that looked like it was made out of leaves and moss. Emily suddenly noticed that two were wearing dresses. She pointed at them. "Those two are girls."

The two female Gnomes curtsied and said hello.

Her mind was going a mile a minute trying to process everything that was going on around her. A noise from behind caught her attention, and turning she saw the one she'd left outside come in through the cat door. "So that's how you got in." Her eyes darted to Zoe who was now being scratched under her chin by The Wise One.

"Traitor. I knew I should have gotten a dog," she cursed.

"Please," The Wise One said pointing to a chair. "Puts a kink in my neck having to look up at you for so long."

She was stunned, dumbfounded, stupefied. She looked wide-eyed at the little creature, trying to sort through all the information that she was gathering in her head. After all, she was a scientist and she didn't know every kind of animal out there. Or she could have actually discovered some unknown species altogether. *They're not any kind of rodent! They're human-like, with understandable speech! They wear clothes and seem civilized! Yeah, I'm not sure what in the heck they are, but I'm up for finding out!* She studied them a moment longer, then sat down slowly on the edge of the wing back chair.

"What I'm about to tell you will be difficult for you to understand. But I beg you to hear me out, then I will answer all your questions. Okay?"

Emily held her hand up.

"What is this gesture?" The Wise One asked. "I do not understand."

"It means I have a question."

"After I'm done explaining why we're here."

"But--."

The Wise One shook his head, "You're like The Young One," he said pointing to the Gnome she had thrown outside. "You need to learn patience."

"*Excuse me!*" she yelled, standing up again.

"Maybe I'm not communicating correctly. Forgive me," he said, with a calming motion.

Emily sat back down grumbling. "I can't believe you come into my house and get attitude with me? I should just kick you right out of here."

"What does that mean?"

"Leave! I should make you leave."

"If we leave, we cannot help you with your quest."

"What quest? What are you talking about?"

The Wise One took a deep breath and then exhaled slowly. "Patience, Emily, I will explain."

Emily was about ready to say something else, but these little beings were intriguing and she wanted to learn more about them. Leaning forward in her seat she said, "I'm all ears, go for it."

He gave her a puzzled looked again. "You appear to consist of more than just ears."

"It's just a saying."

"Does that mean you're ready to listen now?"

"Yes."

The Wise One let out a long sigh, then began again. "The Young One already mentioned Ava."

"The goddess. Which I don't believe in. We had goddesses around here once. It was a long time ago, though. There were three of them, I think. I read something about it in Mythology in eighth grade. But I'm pretty sure none of them were named Ava."

The Wise One glared at her.

"Sorry," she said meekly. "Go on."

Once certain that she was no longer going to interrupt, he continued the story. "Ava is the goddess of *our* planet Terra, which is an exact duplicate of your Valencia, but without humans. She has heard your pleas and has sent us to help you save the animals of your world that are dying under man's hand."

Emily blinked as she looked at the little being. Finally she shook her head, and tried to comprehend what he had just said. "I really want to believe you, but I don't. But I want to because I like your cause, but I can't. See, I'm a scientist and I'm trying to keep an open mind about this, but it can't be true. There is no such thing as people that are a foot tall. I think you guys are a figment of my imagination. You're not real."

From the side, one of the Gnomes moved over to her leg and kicked it.

"Hey, why did you do that?" she said, turning on her assailant.

"I'm not a figment of your imagination. I'm called The Old One. It is a pleasure to meet you, Emily."

"Can we continue now?" The Wise One asked.

Emily absentmindedly rubbed the spot where she'd been kicked, not that it hurt, but more like questioning how it happened if these little things didn't really exist.

"You spoke of science," The Wise One said, shaking his head. "This has nothing to do with science. This is magic. And to understand magic you have to remember what it was like to believe in the impossible."

Emily's elbow slid off her knee. "Magic?"

"Let's see if I can make this easier. Do you know what we are?"

She looked at each of them again. "No."

The Wise One shifted and crossed he arms in front of his chest. "If you were to guess?"

"Elves?"

"Elves are much bigger and have pointy ears," he sighed. "Try again."

Emily studied them again, and then it dawned on her. "You're a Gnome. You look just like that Roaming Gnome on T.V. Well, your clothes are a little different. Yours are a little earthier."

This time The Wise One was at a loss. "I'm sorry, I don't understand this term Roaming Gnome?"

Emily chuckled. "Forget it. It's too hard to explain. You are a Gnome though, right?"

"Yes," he said, collecting his thoughts again. "And Gnomes are?"

"Lawn ornaments."

The Wise One cocked his head and looked at her in disbelief. "Magic. We're magic."

"Oh, okay. I was wondering where you were going with-," Emily was interrupted by a sudden crash. When she looked up and over at her desk, she spotted The Young One dangling over the edge of the desk top hanging onto the computer mouse. "What are you doing?" she asked, standing.

"He has a tendency of getting into-"

"Trouble!"

The Wise One shook his head. "I was going to say *things*. He's curious and likes to explore."

Emily walked over to her desk. "Take that shell off your head," she said, rescuing him from the wire.

"I thought it was some kind of hat. It's very pretty," The Young One said, putting it down on the desk top. "And you have so many."

"It's a shell from a marine gastropod. A type of sea snail." She sat down and looked at the mess on her desk. The Gnome was just inches from her now. "You were into my shell collection."

"I'm very sorry." The Young One bit his bottom lip and looked away from her.

Turning him one way and then the other, Emily studied the little guy intently. He looked a lot like the dolls she had as a child. "There's not much to ya."

"Ow. Hey."

"Did I hurt you?"

"Well kinda," he said, rubbing his arm. "Your fingers are kind of poky."

"But I didn't poke you."

"It doesn't matter, it still hurt, kinda."

"Did it hurt or didn't it?"

"I felt it," he said defensively.

Emily gave him a thoughtful look, then said, "I wonder how you'd do in a maze?"

"What's a maze?"

"It's a path or collection of paths, typically from an entrance to an exit. It's a tool to see if you can solve a puzzle and figure out how to get through without getting lost."

"She's talking about a labyrinth, Young One," The Wise One said from his spot by the door. "And I assure you even that one is smart enough to make it out of a labyrinth."

As Emily watched and studied him, The Young One picked up the mollusk's shell again and placed it back on his head. When he realized that she was watching him he returned it to the desk top. She smiled after studying him a bit longer. "Tegula. That's what kind of mollusk this came from. A Filipe Tegula Snail," she said, putting it back on his head. "And that's what I'm going to call you."

The Young One straightened the shell she had placed on his head, and smiled. "I like both, hat and name. Thank you."

Emily picked Tegula up and moved back over to the chair where she'd been sitting before. He was as tall as some of her Barbie dolls but weighed a lot more. Placing him on the floor in front of her, she sighed and looked over at The Wise One. "Okay, so you really do exist, or this is a really good hallucination."

Tegula laid his hand on her leg. "I'm real. They're real. We're here to help you."

Emily rubbed her face. "I don't understand. Why me? And why now?"

"It was your pleas for help that Ava heard," The Wise One said. "And Terra is ready now for those creatures of your world that need to escape man's cruelty."

Magic wasn't something she could get her head around. From what she knew of the subject, science can explain magic, bur magic can't explain science, or anything else for that matter. But if there was any way that these little guys could help save the animals, she was going

61

to find out. "Okay," she said finally. "Tell me how you're planning on saving the animals?"

"First off," The Wise One said. "Why don't you tell us about these animals we're to be saving?"

Chapter Five

Emily opened her eyes slowly. She had a very stiff and sore neck from the way she'd been laying. Looking around her, she suddenly realized she had fallen asleep on the couch. She was grateful that today was Sunday, and short of an emergency, she wouldn't be going into work.

She'd spent most of the evening explaining the differences between the thousands of endangered, vulnerable, and threatened animals that were listed on her map. For the most part, the Gnomes were very interested in what she was saying, except for Tegula, who kept getting bored and wandering off to explore his surroundings. Earlier in the evening she had found Zoe and him playing on the cat scratching post in the front room. It wasn't until they managed to knock it over and broke the top tier off that Emily had gotten concerned. Later in the evening, she and the others found Tegula outside conversing with a striped skunk on her back porch. Emily managed to get everyone back inside before Tegula's new friend decided it had had enough of the Gnome bothering him. In the early morning hours, she accidently closed him in the refrigerator when she'd opened it to get a beer. The little girl Gnome (which she named Vulpes after *Vulpes riffautae,* an extinct species of fox that she felt the little Gnome looked like) noticed that he was missing, which sparked an immediate search of the home for him, again.

During the search she was told by The Tall One why he and The Young One were getting into the trash in her bathroom, and how the two had taken a liking to chocolate, and how they were the ones who put the teeth marks in them in the first place, and how they had decided that they could get them back after she had thrown them away. He said how he had gotten scared when The Young One fell in, and he tried to run back to the others for help but she had gotten in his way. And how she had scared him even more when she picked The Young One up and threw him outside. And how he was sad because The Young One had forgotten to bring the chocolate back inside with him.

"The trash can is still outside," she said. "Why don't you just go out there and get it?"

The Tall One stopped his search for Tegula and raced outside to retrieve the candy.

Lucky for Tegula, Emily was ready for another beer and found him when she opened the refrigerator again. At first she was startled, but then found the chilled little Gnome quite funny to look at. "Are you okay?" she asked, trying not to laugh.

"I'm used to warmer climate," he said, with a slight shiver. "This room is as cold as the northern icecaps. How is that done?"

The Gnomes were clueless when it came to figuring out compressors, hot gases, and vapor. They were creatures of nature and used to raising and caring for plants and animals, and even with the help of Google Emily couldn't get them to understand the concept of refrigeration.

As a cat owner, Emily often woke in the morning and found herself pinned down by her cat Zoe, but this particular morning she found herself pinned down by one cat and six Gnomes. Besides Tegula and Vulpes, there was *Ptilopsis,* meaning white-faced owl; that was the name she gave The Wise One and with his white hair and beard, she thought he looked kinda like one.

For the one they called The Old One, she named him *Chelonia,* meaning turtle. Chelonia didn't have much hair, and with his wizened face and hocked nose he looked like an old Leatherback turtle she once helped rehabilitate.

Then, of course, there was the one whose running from her bedroom had started the whole fiasco yesterday. The Tall One, he was called by the others, and though he wasn't that much taller than the rest of them, she called him *Masai* after the tallest species of giraffe.

And the last one, a larger, rounder female, quiet and meek; Emily named her after the only animal that she could think of that fit that description. *Sirenia,* for her beloved manatees.

Kicking her feet to loosen the blanket around them, she dislodged a couple of Gnomes and the cat and wiggled her way off the couch. "Stay here," she said sleepily. "I'm going for a run."

Emily quickly changed into a pair of yoga pants and T-shirt. After tying her shoes she went into the bathroom to brush her teeth. Before she knew it, Tegula was sitting on the edge of the sink with his feet dangling inside, watching her. "Would you mind moving your feet," she said with a mouth full of foam.

"What are you doing?"

"Brushing my teeth."

Tegula draw his feet up just as she spit the foam into the sink. "Ewww, does it taste bad?"

Emily took a sip of water from a cup to rinse her mouth then spit that out as well. "No."

"Then why did you spit it out?"

"Because I don't want to swallow it."

"Why not?"

"Because you're not supposed to."

"Why not?"

"Because it can make you sick." She stopped him before he could say anything else, picked him up and set him on the ground. "No more questions. I've got to go for my run."

"What should I do while you're gone?"

Emily grabbed her keys and phone and started for the door. After looking at the bored little Gnome, she took the remote to the T.V. over to him and gave him a crash course on how to use it. On, off, this changes channels, this one's for volume. "Please stay out of trouble. I'm usually only gone about an hour."

When Emily returned home, she found the Ptilopsis and Chelonia sitting on the couch and the younger Gnomes on the floor in front of them, watching the nature channel's Treehouse Builders.

"Quite enjoyable," said Ptilopsis while petting Zoe, who was lying next to him on the couch. "Why don't you ask these men to build you a home in the trees?"

"Don't know if you noticed or not, but there's not a lot of trees around here big enough to hold a house like that," she said, pulling off her jacket. "I'm going to go take a shower."

"Can I come?" Tegula asked, getting to his feet.

"No! I shower alone. Go back to watching T.V."

"But the story is over."

"Find another story to watch." Emily looked at Ptilopsis and Chelonia, "Ah, guys, a little help here?"

Ptilopsis motioned for Tegula to return to his spot. "Sit, Young One, you're making Emily nervous."

Emily made sure that she had locked the door to her bedroom and the bathroom, and then searched everywhere to make sure none of them had gotten in. The last thing she wanted was Tegula or any of the others showing up in her shower asking questions.

After getting dressed and drying her hair, she wandered out of the bedroom. The T.V. was off, everything was clean and there was no sign of the Gnomes. For a brief moment she wondered if last night had just been a really weird dream. She walked farther out into the room until she heard what sounded like weeping coming from her office area. Rounding the corner, she spotted the Gnomes clustered on her desk looking at pictures of the harp seal pup hunts in Farwest.

"Explain, please?" Ptilopsis asked, with a saddened face.

Emily looked at the little Gnomes. Half had tears rolling down their faces. The others just looked totally miserable. Tegula walked over to her as she sat down at her desk. Sitting next to her arm, he rested his hand on it for comfort as she gathered the pictures of the slain seal pups and turned them over so she wouldn't have to look at them, and then slid them back under her keyboard.

"I don't know what to say. It's just another awful thing that man does to animals."

"Why?" Sirenia asked wiped her eyes.

"For their pelts."

"So they use them for clothing?" she asked.

Emily sighed. It was so hard to try to explain the actions of some people. "There was a time when man needed to hunt animals, they used their meat for food, and their skin for clothing, bedding and in some cases to make shelters to protect them from the elements. But we've moved past that now, most of us live in cities or towns. Our homes are made of wood, steel, or stone. We don't have to hunt anymore, animals are raised on farms for us to use as food now. And we no longer need to wear furs for clothing." Emily took a moment to collect her thoughts. "I do a lot of research, read a lot of books, travel, talk to a lot of people, and see things that have changed my life forever. Like the harp seal pups being slain off the coast of Farwest. I went there with my friend Deb about five years ago. Emily pulled a photo album out of her desk drawer, and took the pictures of the seal hunt out from under the keyboard." These are supposed to go in here. This book is full of all kinds of pictures of senseless killings."

Opening the first page she heard a gasp from Sirenia. "The water's red."

"These are photos of the dolphin killings in the Faiji Island. These guys don't eat the dolphin and never have, they just kill the animals because they believe they're eating all the fish in the area and there is a market for the meat over on the mainland. So the fishermen herd the whole pod in to a cove; then, using spikes that sever the spinal cord so they can't swim away, then pull them up into the boats and take them to the market. There've been reports that it can take a long time for an animal to die this way and it will arrive at the market still alive sometimes." Emily flipped the page. "The slaughter of long-finned pilot whales near the Phamoe Islands in the Northern Strait. The village used to need the whale meat to survive, but not anymore. Now, very few people even like the taste of it. The town's elders had to pass a law that each family had to consume a certain portion of the hunt each year so that the tradition of the hunt could go on. They capture the whales when they swim near the islands. They herd them into the shallows with boats and force them to beach. Then the hunters sever their spines with lances, and allow them to bleed out. It's been practiced since around the time the first settlers came to the island."

"Are these some of the animals that we're going to help?" Chelonia asked.

"I'm afraid not. They're not on the endangered species list."

The disappointment on all the Gnomes' faces was obvious. "You're the ones who set the rules, you said only the ones on the endangered list."

Ptilopsis stood and looked at the pictures. There were more, lots more. There was even a section on animal trafficking, with parrots that were being smuggled in plastic bottle, 80 baby iguanas pictured in a cardboard box, a baby orangutan in diapers lying in a plastic crate, a large plastic bag containing thousands of confiscated young eels, long-tailed macaque babies found inside a basket on their way to Topios for sale. Shaking his head, he closed the book and looked thoughtfully at the others.

"It would be best for the animals of this world if we removed the humans from here."

Emily cleared her throat.

"But that's not what we were sent here to do," he said giving her a sympathetic nod. "Beside the animals that we'll be taking to Terra, I believe we can help some of these others by simply helping them avoid humans and those areas in which they would be harmed. Like the long-finned pilot whales, if they don't pass by the islands then they can't be captured, correct?"

"Can you do that?" Emily asked. "I mean, change an animal's migration route or teach them where it's safe to hunt and where it's not?"

"I'm not sure," Ptilopsis said. "But I believe it would be worth the time to find out."

Emily sat in awe.

"When will the whales be scheduled to swim by the islands next?" he asked.

Emily shrugged. "Ah, like now."

77

Emily steadied herself against the rail at the back of the 17 foot speed boat. It had been a couple of years since she had been on board a boat heading out to stop the pilot whale slaughter at the Phamoe Islands in the Northern Straits. While out fishing, a local had spotted 100-150 pilot whales passing by Sinoy (one of the smaller islands on the archipelago). Emily's plan was to get to the whales before the others did, and then let the Gnomes do their thing. Hagen, the boat's owner, was a young man who worked at the salmon farm and had taken a liking to Emily when she had come out with the Sea Guardian's crew to help stop the whale hunt two years ago. Of course, Hagen never knew she was a Sea Guardian, and only knew her as a biologist from Stell, interested in the wildlife in the Phamoe Island region.

Spotting the fins rapidly approaching, Emily opened her backpack and helped Chelonia, and Tegula out. As she moved up beside Hagen, she set the engine to idle and bent him over for a long kiss. With the young man distracted, the Gnomes then disappeared into the water with the whales without being seen.

"I don't understand," he said, as she sat in his lap. "If you just wanted for us to be together, we could have stayed in town."

"You know me, I love being around the whales," she said, tracing a line down his chest.

"The whales make you excited?" he asked, in a confused tone.

"Oh yes, very excited." Emily drew him into another long kiss, stopping only when she noticed that the Gnomes had climbed back on board. "We can go back in now," she said, moving off his lap.

"We can?" he asked, gasping for a breath.

Emily pointed to the other boats approaching. "Looks like it's going to get pretty crowed out here soon."

"Okay," Hagen said, in a haze. "We'll go back to shore."

Emily noticed that the whales had moved away from them and were already way off in the distance swimming in the other direction. While Hagen turned the boat toward shore, Emily went over to help the Gnomes get back into the backpack. She gave them a thumbs up as they climbed in and then she zipped it closed.

Emily agreed to go out with Hagen that night since he was nice enough to take her out in his boat. Leaving the Gnomes in the house they were staying in that night made her a little nervous, but Chelonia ensured her that he could keep The Young One occupied and out of trouble for the time that she'd be away.

Having dinner and a couple of drinks with Hagen wasn't totally bad. He was a really nice guy and it gave them a chance to talk about things like the hunt and the fish farm, and how Sea Guardian was getting people on the mainland to boycott the salmon sales from the islands to save the whales. She'd been away from that organization for a while but it didn't surprise her that they'd use that kind of tactic to sway people toward their cause. Hagen was worried, because if it kept up he would be out of a job soon.

"I'm sure it's all going to work out," she said, touching his arm sympathetically. "The boycott will stop because the whaling is going to stop."

"The whaling has been going on for hundreds of years. What makes you think it'll stop now?"

"Your people don't need the whale meat anymore to survive, they have the salmon and the other fish raised at the farm."

"Yeah, but, it is tradition."

"Faith, Hagen." Emily thought of the Gnomes and smiled. "You've got to have faith in the little things."

Chapter Six

After traveling by ship to Farwest in the morning, Emily and her two companions started making their way back to Toft. Of course, they had a bad scare when Tegula came up missing at the South Point airport and they ended up missing their flight. They finally found him out on the runway trying to get the birds to stay away from the planes.

"Now how are we supposed to get back home?" She asked, frazzled.

"It's dangerous out there, I was trying to get them to understand that the runway is not a good place to nest," he said, as an explanation.

Emily ignored him and continued. "The next direct flight isn't until tomorrow morning, and I don't want to chance losing him in Northern Gondwana with a stop over," she said, looking at the older Gnome.

"Let's try this," Chelonia said. "Picture where you want to go and we'll take you there."

Emily looked at the old Gnome in disbelief. "What! You can just blink and we're there?"

"Wel--"

"Why didn't you tell me this before?"

"Wel--"

"I can't believe you had us travel halfway around the world, and I missed 2 days of work, and you let me spend a pretty big chunk of my life savings on plane tickets that I didn't even need, when you could have just zapped us there and back in a blink of an eye." Emily looked at him in frustration. "What are you waiting for?"

"First of all, I'm not sure if it'll work. Secondly, we need a clear picture."

"You know what my house looks like."

"It needs to be you," Chelonia said calmly. Taking The Young One's hand, he touched Emily's arm. "Think of home."

"Wow," Tegula shouted, standing at the top of the rock cliff and looking out over the water. "This is beautiful. Hey look, I see whales out there."

"Where are we?" Chelonia asked, in a stupefied tone.

Emily stood there dumbfounded. "How did you do that?"

"It's an ability that the goddess gave us to move around our planet. I believe you know it as magic."

"Magic," Emily shook her head. "Science exists, magic doesn't."

"Then how did we get here, and where is here?" Chelonia asked

"I must be dreaming, but this really does look like Black Rock Lighthouse on the northern tip of Gondwana."

"I don't understand, I told you to think of home."

Emily shrugged. "I'm a scientist, I didn't believe you could just pop us in and out of places. I guess you can though." She sat down on the rocks and studied the pod of whales swimming off shore.

Tegula sat down next to her. "I have a feeling that you are going to miss them, aren't you?"

Emily nodded. "I have a couple of adoption certificates at home buried away somewhere. I got them when I was a little kid and my aunt first took me to the whale museum at in Stell. Ruffle NS41 and Hana NS79. Lost Hana in 2013 and Ruffle in 2014. They both just went missing." She looked over at Tegula and Chelonia who were sitting next to each other.

"That's what's going to happen if and when we send the whales away. There's going to be a lot of people worried sick about them. Not knowing if they're dead or alive. These guys aren't like the pilot whales that we dealt with yesterday. These all have names and numbers. There's people out there who have been studying them for over fifty years. They're going to be missed. I mean, truly missed."

Emily drew her knees up to her chest and buried her face in her arms and started crying. When next she looked up, she spotted spray just a few feet from the rocks below her. Standing she saw Tegula and Chelonia at the bottom, chatting with the whales. Climbing down the wall of rocks, she noticed which whale was closest to the Gnomes. "Oh my god," she exclaimed. "Are you talking to her?"

Stopping a few feet away, Emily tried to maintain her cool. It was illegal for her to be this close to an endangered animal. Sitting down, she looked anxiously at the Gnomes. Speaking loudly so they could hear her, she said, "We call her Nanna NS2. She's the oldest whale that we know of in the Northern Straits."

"Yes," Chelonia said, as he started climbing back up to her. "She told us that she's been in these waters a long time."

"Did you tell her about Terra?" Emily asked, feeling her throat starting to tighten again.

"Yes, she's not against taking her kind into clean water with an abundance of fish."

Even though she was too far away to matter, she instinctively reached out to stop Tegula as he leaped off the rocks into the water among the whales. "What is he doing?"

"There's babies out there who have never seen a Gnome and want to play." Chelonia moved next to her and sat down. "We'll let them play for a while, then we'll head home."

"This is really happening isn't it?"

Chelonia nodded.

Emily cringed when she saw Tegula tossed about four feet into the air by one of the babies. "Oh my, I hope they don't kill him."

"He's tougher than he looks and a pretty good swimmer, and besides the old one said she would keep an eye him."

"Did she say how old she is? I mean, we think she's over a hundred but were not sure. She was captured with the rest of her pod in 70's but was deemed too old at that time for a marine park, so she was released."

"She didn't say in years how old she was, only that she remembers a time when man would come out onto the water in smaller boats and would move quietly amongst them."

A smile came to Emily as she thought about what it must have been like to be a native back in those days and have that kind of relationship they had with the whales.

They waited about twenty minutes for Tegula to tire of playing and say good-bye to his new friends. After he dragged himself back up the rocks to where they were sitting, Emily took his and Chelonia's hands and said, "Okay boys, let's go home."

A goddess knows no time. It seemed like only yesterday that she had been here, but something about her surroundings told her that she'd been gone a very, very long time. Cathleena passed through the thick brush of the southeastern side of the Farwest Plains to a clearing where one of her precious Black Rhinoceros lay dying. Its horns had been hastily sawed off, and the poachers had left it for dead. Placing a hand on its side, she released it from its pain, returned the beast to the earth, and covered it with thick green vegetation that its kind like to eat. Not far away she found another, then another. Five in all she sent back to the earth where their bodies would start the cycle of life all over again. There were no other animals in sight, and none that she could sense. Sorrowful, she started to wander aimlessly, and soon found herself in a bank of thick fog which surrounded her with a sense of peace.

As the mist thinned, a spot of startlingly clean sunlight shone through. She made her way there and peered out into a large, grassy clearing. On the opposite side was the dazzling white marble pavilion where she and her sisters once ruled over this world. Moving gracefully to the steps, she ascended and stood where she had often seen her older sister Adele stand with flaming red hair to watch over the humans of Valencia.

What she saw was disturbing to say the least. The carnage was horrible, the butchery of the animals, her animals, dead, dying, their habitats destroyed. And most of her beautiful forests gone. No safe havens for the beast, none at all. Man was everywhere, encroaching on their very existence, and even killing each other. She wished at that moment that her sister Zorine was there with her to cast down the rain, thunder, and lighting to send the pathetic humans scurrying for shelter. She didn't have Zorine though, she only had herself. And it was enough. Calling on the might of the earth itself, she poured all of her agony, anguish, and anger into it and caused the ground to shake like it had never shaken before. Vast sections of cities shook, buildings crumbled, thousands of people were buried under rubble and rock. Closer to the coast, the earth opened up, swallowing whole towns. Ships out to sea and in dock sank under the mighty waves. "Look what you're doing to your world!" her scream thundered across the sky. "You're so stupid, you don't even realize you're destroying it. And what will you have once it's gone? Have any of you ever thought about that?"

Her words were caught by the wind she'd created, and spent over a world that was no longer listening. Cathleena stumbled back away from the edge of her rage, and calmed herself and the earth.

With no one to govern the humans, there was no way to stop them. Valencia was no longer her concern, according to her father. *Her father*, she thought bitterly. This was a forgotten realm for him. She had to hope that he wouldn't learn of her harming the humans just now. But she couldn't just let the animals suffer at man's hand. She tried to think of what Adele would do and decided that she'd have to remove the animals before she could fix the problem with the humans. She needed help, though. *Who on this forsaken plant can I call upon?* Moving back to the edge, she caught sight of a light amongst the rubble. Looking closer, she spotted a small child in her bed, safe and unharmed. "You are a special one," the goddess said, reaching out and touching a mark on the little girl's chest. "You will be my champion, and with you we will save the animals of this world. And eventually the whole planet."

"Explain?" Ptilopsis asked.

Emily pushed herself away from her desk where her and the Gnomes where trying to decide which animal should go to Terra first. All of sudden, the subject of Ava came up, and then of course, it led to the remarks that Emily made earlier about Valencia's deities. Emily went to her book case and came back with an old black and silver school book. Opening it, she read the first page

aloud. "The magical world in which the ancient

Valencia's goddesses ruled, was a world full of fights,

bickering, wars, compromise, fear, fun, love, and

punishment. Many myths were based on the fact that the

goddesses, like mortal men, could be punished for their

actions. Valencian mythology is a collection of myths and

teachings that belong to the ancient Valencians concerning

their deities. Modern scholars refer to and study the myths

in an attempt to shed light on the religious and political

institutions of Ancient Valencia and its civilization of the

time."

"So they tried to teach you something about them,"

Ptilopsis said, rubbing his chin.

"Nobody believes this stuff, that's why it's called a

myth. It's just a story. A made up story."

"You seem to believe it. Or at least you want to believe it."

"No I don't."

"Then how was your world created?"

"Well…there's this big bang theory, but it's a little hard to explain."

Ptilopsis shook his head in disappointment. "Jabaz created all worlds, then left them to his offspring to rule over. Hence Ava with Terra, and Cathleena and her sisters with Valencia. It's all about magic."

"Sorry, but I just don't believe in divine beings. But if you want to meet someone who's a firm believer, I can introduce you to my friend Deb."

"Explain?" Ptilopsis said.

"Why do you keep saying that?"

"Because I want to understand. Why her and not you?"

"Deb's parents are into Archaeology, all they do is look for religious artifacts to help them understand the deities of ancient Valencia. They were working on a dig they called the Sacred Valley. It's on the outskirts of the High Reaches Mountains nestled in the eastern section of the Forest of Shadows. Among all the other things, they unburied a little village up there that had a shrine to the goddess Cathleena. Well, at least they think that's what it was, because there was a shrine and it had animal carvings all around it. Anyway, they took Deb up there all the time in the summers when we were little, and she believes in all that stuff. They estimated that the shrine and village was thousands of years old."

"So she learned from her parents about the goddesses. Do not your parents believe?"

Emily's face saddened, "My folks were killed in the great quake. I was raised by an aunt in Gondwana, and no, she wasn't a believer."

Ptilopsis nodded. "This place that you spoke of, the one that your friend Deb went to. Can you take me there?"

"I've never been there," she stammered, "But I do have a picture of it that Deb gave me back in the eighth grade. I think that was the last year she went there with her parents." Emily dug out the picture and showed it to Ptilopsis.

Touching Emily's arm, he smiled at her. "Put the picture in your mind. Let's use a little magic and see what happens."

The Sacred Valley was roughly 60 square miles in an area of dense forest that's normally very hard to get to. The whole place was being overtaken by the forest once more, and it was dark, wet and eerie to her. She watched from the sideline as Ptilopsis moved around and through the ruins. The afternoon air had a chill to it, and most of the archaeological site was in the shade. Then suddenly, without warning, a large bird swooped down and perched itself on a small stone structure about twenty feet from her. To Emily's surprise, it was a Northern White-faced Owl, the very bird she had named the Gnome after.

Emily closed the distance between her and the bird. The Gnome was already there, and seemed to be conversing with it. Drawn to the small structure, she studied it intently, running her fingers along the hieroglyphs and stopping at a symbol of a wolf's or dog's paw. She took a picture of it with her phone so she could look up the symbols later.

She looked at Ptilopsis. Getting his attention, she pointed at the carving where the paw was, and then lowered the collar of her shirt to show him the mark on her chest near her collar bone. "There seems to be more about you than first believed," he said.

"What does it mean?"

The owl hooted and fluttered his wings.

"He says you've been touched by the gods," Ptilopsis replied.

Emily went and sat on a low wall which encircled the shrine. "Deb said the same thing to me once. I got mad and threatened to clobber her."

"I know this is hard for you to believe." Ptilopsis sat down next to her. "Why don't you tell me about the three? What you remember from school."

"There were three sisters. Zorine, the oldest, was the goddess of the elements. Adele looked over the humans, and Cathleena, the youngest, was the goddess of nature. According to Deb's dad, there used to be shrines like this all over the world. People would pray to Cathleena for a good hunt or harvest. If they needed rain or the wind to cool a hot summer's day, they would pray to Zorine. And Adele would bless them with children or bring comfort to the sick and dying.

Emily rocked back and forth on the wall, then looked over at Ptilopsis, "I don't feel so good. This place is really creeping me out. Can we go home now?"

He nodded and moved over to her side.

"What does all this mean?" she asked.

"I don't know," he said touching her arm. "But I have a feeling we're going to find out."

Ava was young and still learning, but her movements were becoming more graceful. The elegant floating motion of a goddess was just beyond her grasp, but she still gave it a try and managed to move across the pavilion to her sister's side without tripping.

Cathleena held back a smile and acknowledged her sibling. It had been a long time since more than just one of Jabaz's offspring had stood on the huge marble slab that was the floor of her white pavilion. On one hand, it brought her great pleasure, and on the other, great sorrow. She missed her older sister. *Even Zorine, though she could be a tyrant at times. And it's sad that Ava never got to know Adele, she would have liked her, I'm sure,* she thought.

"Tonight you will set the events into motion?" Ava asked.

"Yes."

"Now we will learn if this champion of your is up to the task."

"Do you doubt?" Cathleena asked, looking out over her world, watching Emily and The Wise One enter the village.

"No, sister." Ava looked out at the scene before them. "What is that place?"

Cathleena moved her hand in front of them as if erasing the scene they were watching and replacing it with a new one, but it wasn't new, it was actually one from the past. The buildings were whole once again with people and animals moving all around. An old man made his way through the busy streets winding around the horse drawn carts, and vendors were talking and mingling with the villagers.

"Who is that?"

"My first champion," Cathleena said, her face saddening. "He was always dissing his mother, stopping the hunt, taking food from the humans' tables. But then she would give it right back to them. It used to make him so angry."

"I…I don't understand?"

"This was Adele's oldest. Sabvon. He was always saving the animals from mankind, even as a child. As he grew, he worked to get people to see animals as partners, not possessions. They used to call him a Beastmaster, for he could talk to, and was friends with any and all creatures." Cathleena heaved a sigh, then continued. "But it wasn't just the animals that he cared about, he loved all of nature. He helped teach people to replace what they used for future generations. If lumber was taken from the forest to build with, saplings were planted to replace them. For every tree taken, five were put in its place. He built the temple in his village to communicate with me. I miss our talks." Cathleena stepped away from the edge, allowing the image of her nephew to fade. "This is how I last saw him."

Ava turned and watched her sister move to the three thrones on the opposite side of the pavilion, where the rulers of Valenica once sat. After an agonizing moment, she sat in the middle seat and said. "I will go to Emily tonight and tell her of our plan.

"Then I will go and make sure everything is ready for our first arrivals." As Ava was turning to leave, she stopped and looked back at Cathleena. "There's something about Emily that you're not telling me?"

Cathleena placed her hands on the arms of the throne and straightened her posture. "I believe she could be descended from his line."

"Sabvon's?"

Cathleena nodded. "She bears a mark I believe to be his."

Ava cocked her head and smiled. "A child from Adele's line... Could it truly be?"

Chapter Seven

Emily woke from a restless sleep and ran out to her desk. Inevitably, with the light going on, she woke the Gnomes from their sleeping spots around the front room, as her eyes adjusted, she found the spot on the map and placed her finger on it.

"Good morning," Tegula yawned, as he sat on the desk rubbing his eyes.

"Sorry little buddy," she said, touching his cheek. "It's not morning yet,"

"Why are we up then?"

"We're going to go save some whales."

"Explain," Ptilopsis grumbled, as he climbed up on to the desk.

"I had a dream," she said with excitement. "Well, I think it was a dream. Anyway, in my dream I was told to hurry to the Faiji Islands, you remember the place where we saved the dolphins?"

Ptilopsis nodded with a yawn. They had told the dolphins in that area to stay away from the islands, like they did with the pilot whales in the north, so that the humans wouldn't hurt them anymore, and it seemed to be working.

"They're planning a big whale hunt," Emily said. "The Panthalassan and the Faijien are planning to hit a group of migrating Southern Sea Right whales as they come up the southern straits, between Panthalassa and the Faiji Islands today. We've got to save them." Emily stopped and looked at the Gnomes with dire concern in her eyes. "The humans don't know it, but they're the last of their kind."

This was going to be their first attempt to actually move an animal from one world to the other. The theory was similar to them moving Emily from one place to the other. All Emily had to do was be in contact with one of the whales and a Gnome and picture Terra, which was basically Valencia without man or his influences. Because she was in such a rush, they didn't get a chance to put their theory to the test.

"Nothing like running an experiment in the field," she laughed. "Besides, what's the worst that can happen?"

Ptilopsis thought for a moment. "We could end up somewhere other than Terra."

Emily sighed. "I wasn't really expecting you to say that."

He gave her an apologetic shrug.

Since Emily had been to the Faiji Islands before, getting there was fairly easy; the tough part was getting out to the water. Because of the culture clash, foreigners weren't always welcomed in Faiji or, for that matter, in any of the smaller islands in the archipelago. After wasting a lot of time, Emily finally found a shrimper that was going out for the day. Weaving an elaborate story, she convinced the man that she knew exactly where the shrimp would be that day, and offered to pay him double what he would have made if he'd just gone out on his own. The man had no problem with taking Emily out to the southern straits.

Standing at the bow of the thirty-seven foot shrimp boat with the wind in her hair, she stared out into pre-morning sky. Off in the east the sky was just starting to turn pink. She felt Tegula move up to the railing in front of her. "I can sense you're scared, why?"

"There's going to be bigger ships than us out here," she said. "The Sea Guardian lost a ship last year to the whaling fleet out of Faiji. Three people went down with that ship. The Faijien are fierce, and it'll be better if we get the whales and get out of there before they see us."

Even after handing the captain a couple hundred in cash, it took a lot for Emily to keep him on course. Even she knew that shrimp were never found this far out into the straits, but they hadn't come across the whales yet. In her dream the sun was fully up. She waited nervously for that to be the case here.

The Gnomes, all six of them, were on board and hiding in different places around the deck. Only Tegula stayed out with Emily, using her body to block the captain's view of him from the wheel house.

After another hour into the trip, the captain shouted to Emily about heading back to shore again, and this time he put action to words and started turning the boat to head back to Faiji. Facing the wheel house to argue with him, she spotted in the dim early morning light a fleet of larger ships coming up from behind. And in between them and the fleet were the Right Whales. "Oh no, they're behind us. We need to get between the fleet and the whales," she gasped.

Tegula touched her leg and in the next instant they were exactly where Emily said she wanted to be, between the fleet and the whales. Unfortunately they were closer to the fleet and directly in front of them at a dead stop. Emily screamed and grabbed Tegula, as the first, but luckily for them the smallest, of the Faijien ships in the fleet slammed into the back of their vessel, pushing it down and to the side.

Everything happened so quickly, and even though she hit her head on the railing as she was thrown overboard, she didn't get knocked out. As she tumbled through the water, she keep hearing someone in her head say *take them to Terra, take them to Terra*. Emily felt something surge up underneath her.

Ptilopsis patted her hand and kept calling her name. Emily was sure she was still asleep in bed and that it was way too early to be getting up. She could hear him, and feel him, but she had no desire to open her eyes and look at him. Finally, she stirred and moved her hand to her face. Her head started to throb at her touch.

"She's got to wake up," she heard Tegula say. "She's just got to."

Emily thought to herself that he sounded very sad and upset, and that she should console him. She tried to clear her aching head, putting her hands down beside her body she used them to lever herself up. Whatever she was sitting on felt like a peeled hard-boiled egg. Opening her eyes she looked down at her legs. "This is so cool," she said, once she realized she was sitting on the back of one of the whales, and not in her bed.

"Welcome to Terra," Ptilopsis said, patting her hand one more time. "You gave us a bit of a scare."

Emily touched her head gingerly. "What happened?"

"You saved the whales," Sirenia said, pointing to the water around them. "There's almost two hundred of them."

Emily looked out over the pod of resting mammals. Patting the whale underneath her she said. "I've never been this close to something this big. And I'd be really excited about it, if I didn't feel so bad right now."

She laid back down and groaned, "They don't have aspirin on Terra, do they?"

"No, I'm sorry they don't," Ptilopsis said, touching her shoulder. "I think it's time we get you back to Valencia and get you some help. Sirenia will stay with the whales, and get them settled into their new home. It shouldn't take too long."

Emily tried to sit up again, but thought better of it when she started seeing stars.

"It's okay Em, I'll take care of you," Tegula said, settling down next to her and giving her a hug. "Do you think that man is going to be mad that we sank his boat?" he whispered.

"Oh, I'm sure we made a lot of people mad at us today." Then she fainted.

"Ah, you're awake. Nine stiches and a concussion, not bad for your first rescue mission," Chelonia said, sitting next to her on the bed. "You're all over the story box. It's quite exciting."

Chelonia held up the remote and started to flick through the channels. "The sinking of a small shrimping boat by the Faijien whaling fleet was big news. Oh, and by the way, the owner of the shrimp boat is safe and unharmed. He was lucky enough to get picked up by one of the whaling ships after his vessel went down. The gentleman is claiming that he saw no whales, and is very worried about you, telling everyone that they needed to be looking for the poor woman that went overboard when his boat was struck and sunk. He also said something about his fellow countrymen drinking too much sake before leaving port."

Emily gave a feeble laugh, then asked as she looked around. "Ah, where am I? Where's Tegula, Ptilopsis and the others?"

"They are at home. We felt it would be best if just I stayed with you while you were in the hospital." Chelonia glanced up at her. "Tegula acted hastily and caused you to get injured. Ptilopsis is not happy with him. He won't be coming to visit."

Emily turned the volume down so she could concentrate. "That's not fair. I told him that we needed to get between the whalers and the whales," she said, catching his gaze. "He shouldn't be punished for that."

Chelonia stood. "I will pass on your concern to The Wise One." With that he disappeared, leaving Emily lost on his actions until a nurse showed up to take her vitals.

"What's your name?" the old woman asked, as she shined a light into her eyes.

"Emily."

"What month is this?"

"June."

"Do you know what day it is?"

"Depends, how long have I been here, and where is here?"

"You're in Harmany, you were brought in yesterday morning."

"Harmany, Panthalassa? Yesterday, why did they bring me here?"

"I don't know if you know this or not sweetie, but you were in a bad boating accident."

"Yeah, I remember, I just don't understand why they brought me here instead of taking me home."

The nurse looked at her questionably. "The paramedics brought you here because we're the closest hospital to the beach where you were found. It wouldn't have been safe for you to just go straight home. Not after taking a blow to the head like you did. If nothing else, we needed to stitch up that gash on your forehead."

"I'm talking about the Gnomes," she said angrily. "Why didn't they take me home? They asked me and I told them I wanted to. Why am I here?"

"I'm going to go talk to the doctor, maybe we should get a picture of that head of yours. Are you hungry, dear? I'll have them send some food up for you."

Emily watched as the nurse backed out of the room. Once she was gone, Chelonia reappeared. "Why didn't you take me home?" she asked.

"You couldn't give us a clear picture, we barely got you here. I mean, back to Valencia," he whispered as he disappeared again.

Emily turned the sound up and tried to focus on the T.V. She still had a bit of a headache and now that she was sitting up more she was starting to feel nauseous. Sliding back down in the bed, she spotted a hooded figure near the door. "My name is Emily Dickens, it's Tuesday June 14th, and I'd like to go home now," she said turning her head towards it.

"I wasn't sure I should intervene, but this way will take too long."

Emily's hand went to her chest as she gazed upon the woman who had entered her room. Since when did nurses wear long hooded robes? The voice she was sure she had heard before. But when, and where? "Do I know you?" she asked, hesitantly.

The woman moved forward as if floating on air. Reaching out, she gently touched the wound on Emily's head, causing it to disappear instantly. The next thing Emily knew she was sitting in her chair at home with the younger Gnomes scurrying around the house, seeing to her every need. Ptilopsis and Chelonia, on the other hand, were studying the map of endangered animals.

"What just happened?" she asked out loud, watching the Gnomes move about.

"Here's your phone," Tegula said, holding it out to her.

Emily took it absentmindedly.

"It got a little wet when you went into the water. I laid it out in the sun, to dry it. But I don't think it worked."

Emily glanced at the phone, and tried to turn it on.

"It's broken isn't it?" he moaned.

"It was time for a new one anyway," she said, pulling him onto her lap. "I'm like, two upgrades behind. I'll go down to the mall tomorrow and get another one. It's okay."

"You're not mad?"

Emily shook her head.

Catching his attention, she asked. "Did we save the whales?"

"Yes, don't you remember?"

"Not really. I think I might have hit my head when I went into the water."

"You did."

"Well, that explains the weird dream I had."

"What dream?"

"Well, in one I was in a hospital and this strange lady healed a gash that I had on my head."

"That wasn't a dream."

"Was that the goddess, Ava?"

"No. That was your goddess, Cathleena," he said. "She helped us get you back to Valencia."

"I don't understand," she said, in a bewildered tone.

"Things didn't go the way they were supposed to. You kept wanting to sleep. We couldn't get you to concentrate on home. Cathleena came to take you back."

"Back?"

"Home, to Valencia."

Emily noticed the two older Gnomes had stopped talking and were looking her way. Meeting their gaze, she hesitated a moment before going over to join them. "I'll be right back," she said, moving Tegula off her lap.

"Are you feeling better?" Chelonia asked.

"Yeah," Emily said, automatically touching her head. "It doesn't hurt anymore."

"Good," Ptilopsis said. Turning back to the map, he added, "You had us worried there for a time."

Emily stood nervously for a moment, then finally said. "I don't believe in her."

"In who?" Ptilopsis asked.

"Cathleena. I don't believe in her. It must have been someone else who came to the hospital."

Ptilopsis turned to face her. "It was Cathleena."

"Why would she help me?"

"That's a good question," he said, sitting down on the desk. "Maybe because she believes in you?"

Emily was taking what Ptilopsis just said into consideration when Chelonia interrupted her thoughts with a question of his own. "Do you know much about this animal?"

"I'm not done with this conversation," she said to Ptilopsis, before turning her attention to what Chelonia was pointing at. "Yeah, that's the Black Rhino."

"Go on."

"How much do you want to know?"

Chelonia shrugged. "Everything you know."

Emily sighed, then continued. "The Black Rhino can be identified by their pointed upper lip, they're browsers that eat mostly small trees and bushes. They're solitary animals, and reproduce every two to five years, single calf that stays with its mother for about three years. They like to eat at night when it's cooler, and stay in the shade during the day. Their downfall is their horns, which are revered for medicinal uses in Topios, and Faiji. The horns are also valued in Central Hamur and the Garlain Plains as an ornamental dagger handle," she said, pointing to a part of the map. "They used to roam most of Farwest Plains, but these days take refuge in the thickets in the Southeastern section of the plains. The thorny bushes there don't bother the Rhino's thick armored skin and it makes it harder for the poacher to get to them."

"Used to," Ptilopsis said sorrowfully. "The humans have found a way to get in. There's not many of these rhinos left now."

"How do you know that?"

"We were asked to make them a priority."

"By who, Ava?"

"By Cathleena."

"Of course. Cathleena."

"Why is it so easy for you to believe in Ava, but not your own Goddess Cathleena?"

Emily shrugged, unable to put her tormented feeling into words. *Why was it easier to believe in Ava?* She asked herself. Maybe because she knew nothing about her. Everything that she read about Valencia's goddesses wasn't good. Ava didn't abandon her world, she was trying to help save theirs. Deb's father told them that according to the old text, even after Adele's banishment, that Cathleena and Zorine had control of Valencia. That it could have worked out with just the two of them. They could have kept the balance between man and nature. But they didn't, they gave up and left Valencia to the destructive hands of man, and their false gods like Fortuna, Marduk, and Baal.

"The Black Rhino," Chelonia said. "Can you find them?"

Emily took a deep breath to clear her head, *I'm here for the animals,* she told herself. Sitting down at the computer, she pulled up what files she had on the rhinos, and like all her files it held disturbing pictures of dead and mutilated carcasses, all with no horns.

"Can you take us there?" Chelonia asked as the other Gnomes gathered around them.

Emily studied the background in the picture, then felt a little hand touch her shoulder. In seconds a hot dry heat swept over them. There was barely time to catch their breath when she heard gunfire erupt all around her, forcing her to the ground. "Dang it, someone's shooting at us," she yelled.

Tegula moved alongside her and pointed behind them. "I think they were shooting at them."

She'd seen dead animals many times, but never a human being before. Two males, darker skin color than hers, but around her own age, and by their clothing she could see they were some kind of ranger or soldier. She looked away and into Tegula's face. The shooting seemed to have stopped, and was now replaced by sound of heavy equipment. "What is that?" she asked in horror.

Tegula scrambled into the bushes. After a minute, he returned and waved her toward him. "There's a bunch of them, they're coming from all sides. They have several rhinoceros trapped in the middle."

After dozens of scratches and scrapes and tears in her clothes and skin, she finally crawled through the thickets to a spot where she could see what was happening. "We've got to get between the rhinos and the bulldozers," she said, grabbing Tegula's shoulder.

"No, you got hurt the last time we did that."

Emily heard a gunshot and turned to see one of the rhinos fall. "We've got to do it now," she shouted.

"Yes," Ptilopsis said, appearing out of nowhere, "We must act quickly. Emily, take us to the rhinos, and then to Terra," he said touching her arm.

Man. No man, it was getting a little easier. Emily sat with her hand resting on the downed rhino. Around her stood the other rhinos with the six Gnomes milling amongst them. Unfortunately, the one her hand rested on was now dead.

"It's okay," Vulpes said, placing her hand beside hers. "This one was old, he gave his life to save the others."

"At least they didn't get his horn," Emily said choking back tears and brushing herself off.

Looking out into the crash of rhinoceros she saw a bunch of cows and a young calf, but only one other bull besides the dead one next to her.

"There's so few."

"Terra has its own Black Rhinoceros," Vulpes said. "Soon these will mix in with those in the west. I'll stay with them for a while to get them on the right path to their new home."

She felt drained from the stress and for a brief moment thought about the poor men who had died trying to save these rhinos. *If only I'd gotten there a little sooner.* Emily heaved a heavy sigh, and watched the rhinoceros follow Vulpes into a large shaded area not far away.

"Are you ready to go home?"

"Yeah, I guess so," she said standing. "Who's up for pizza?"

"Me, I think," Tegula said, latching onto her leg.

"Explain, please?" Ptilopsis asked, moving up next to her. "What is pizza?"

"It's a comfort food. And I really need some comfort food right now."

Chapter Eight

Emily almost choked on the piece of pizza she was eating, she was laughing so hard, watching six little Gnomes munching down, and drinking something they'd never tasted before, sauce all over their face and hands, belching, and burbling. It was the funniest thing she'd ever seen. She had ordered a two liter of pop and a medium vegetarian pizza so as not to offend anyone. It seemed to be a hit. Vulpes had gotten back just in time for the pizza party and quickly ran to get herself a piece. Emily ended up cursing herself for ruining her phone, she would have loved to been able to take a picture of the celebration.

She sat down next to Ptilopsis and Zoe on the couch. The little Gnome was eating with one hand, petting Zoe with the other, and getting cat fur all over his food. It didn't seem to bother him, and Zoe was purring with a smug expression on her face. "She's really taken a liking to you," Emily said to the Gnome.

"I like her--" Before he finished his sentence, Ptilopsis disappeared, and his piece of pizza dropped onto the couch where he'd been sitting.

Emily quickly looked around her. All the Gnomes were gone. Her mind started racing. A knock on the door startled her, then she realized that was the reason for the Gnome's disappearances. "Just a minute," she called out, picking up the pizza slices that had been left all around her living room from her little guests.

"Come on Em, let me in."

Emily hesitated a moment, and then ran to the door and yanked it open. "Deb?" she said in dismay.

Deb locked her arms around her and gave her a big hug. When Emily cringed she let up. "I'm sorry, did I hurt you? Dang you Em, I've been so worried about you." Deb moved into the house and was about ready to throw her suitcase on the couch when she saw all the food. "You having a party?"

Emily snagged one of the pizza slices and sat down. "No, it's just me. Do you want a piece?" she said handing her a slice that hadn't been chewed on.

"Ah--okay," Deb said, as she hesitantly accepted the food.

"So what are you doing here?" Emily asked.

"What am I doing here? You don't show up for work. No one has heard from you for days. Then they find out on the news that you were on a ship that went down in the Straits. You're not answering your phone.

They finally find the hospital that you were sent to, but guess what, you're missing from there too, so who do they call?"

"Who called you?"

"Your work. You put me down as an emergency contact."

"I did?"

Emily looked distant and lost in thought, Deb shook her arm to get her attention. "You okay?"

Emily met her friend's gaze. There was so much she wanted to tell her, but knew she couldn't. With a sigh, she held her hand out. "Can I use your phone to call work? Mine kinda got wet."

"So what did they say?" Deb asked, grabbing another piece of pizza.

Emily handed her phone back to her. "They put me on a leave of absence. Good thing I have money in savings."

"Being on leave, is that good or bad?"

Emily shrugged and walked over to her desk. "I guess it's good, I've got a lot on my plate right now. I can use the time off." She felt her friend staring at her. "What?"

Deb crossed her arms in front of her chest. "Are you going to tell me what's been going on here? They told me you were on death's door, and I get here and there's not a mark on you. But you are acting kinda weird."

"I'm fine. They over-exaggerated my injuries. I got a little bump on the head." Emily saw a couple of Gnomes popping in and out, grabbing pizza and their glasses of pop. She started chuckling until she saw Ptilopsis urging her to follow. "Gotta pee, I'll be right back."

Ptilopsis shut the door to the bathroom behind her after she entered. "She can't see us."

"She physically can't? Or you just don't want her to see you?"

"At this time it is unwise for her to."

"But she's my friend, and she believes in all this stuff."

"Sorry. It doesn't matter."

"So what if I tell her about you anyway?" Emily said, in frustration.

"Would she believe you?"

"Of course she would."

Ptilopsis gave her a doubtful look. "The decision is up to you."

Emily studied him a moment and then left the bathroom. "You up for a drive?" she asked Deb when she re-entered the room where she had left her. "Thought I'd show you some of things I've been doing down here."

"Okay, here it comes, don't move, don't move," Emily repeated as the creature closed the distance between them. By the time Deb could turn completely around, the gentle giant, that Emily guessed was a female from what little she could see, was only a few feet away. For the next few minutes, the animal circled them. Both women remained quiet and still, more from amazement than anything else. Emily put her snorkel and mask on and signaled Deb to do the same. Dipping below the surface, the two humans immersed themselves into the wet and wonderful world of the manatee. A world unlike their own; blue, sodden, and sprinkled with a variety of different sized and colored fish that darted between the light and the shadows cast all around them by the vegetation overhead.

It was very calming and relaxing, and at that moment neither woman had a worry in the world. As they floated there, they were truly awestruck by the majestic and beautiful beast that passed slowly by them.

The manatee approached and made eye contact with them both, then came closer to Emily. She smiled with her eyes as the manatee's fin ever so gently touched her shoulder. She locked eyes with Deb trying to hold back tears of joy and amazement, and at that moment, she fell in love all over again with these beautiful creatures, and swore that someday she'd be sending them to Terra, away from the evil people of this world who wanted to hurt them.

As the animal swam away, the two women surfaced. Deb couldn't stop smiling. "That was the best."

Emily nodded and pointed around them. "Look who snuck up on us when we weren't looking."

All that time they had been focusing on the lone female, they were being surrounded by dozens of other manatees. Deb's excitement was apparent as she dropped back under the water.

They spent the afternoon becoming one with nature. Watching all kinds of wildlife, bald eagles, dolphins, otters, and raccoons on the water's edge. There was also a large array of local waterfowl; egrets, herons, ducks, geese, pelicans, cranes, but by far the best part of the day was swimming among the manatees. As the sun started going down, they called it a day and climbed out onto the rented pontoon boat, and headed back to the dock.

"That was an incredible experience," Deb said, as she worked off her wet suit. "I've only seen pictures of them."

Emily thought for a moment as she tossed her equipment into the back of her truck. "If there was one animal on the endangered species list that you could personally save, which one would it be?"

Deb tossed her things into the truck and climbed up on the tail gate. "That's not fair, I'd want to save them all."

"I know, but say, if you could personally save one, who would it be?"

"The orcas in the Northern Straits."

"No, I already picked those, you have to pick something else."

Deb thought for a moment. "I can't think of anything else. I don't remember everything on the list."

Emily thought for a moment. "Let's grab something to eat," she said, pulling out her keys. "Then we'll head back to my place. I have a map with all the endangered species listed on it."

"How's the sushi out here?" Deb asked, as she headed for the cab of the truck.

Emily shrugged. "Not as good as back home, but it's okay."

Emily got on her computer as Deb studied the map. "I didn't realize there were so many now."

"There's roughly 3100 animal and 2600 plant species listed that are near extinction," Emily said, as she typed on the keyboard. "That's up 188 from last year.

Deb shook her head, "That is sick. And most people don't even know there's a problem."

Emily sighed. Pulling an animal up on the screen, she said. "What about this one? I know you were kind of fond of them when we were kids. You got really mad when they sent Poa and Chi to that elephant refuge."

Deb looked at the picture of the Farwest Elephant. "Chi and Poa were Garlain Plains Elephants. Wato was the one from the Farwest Plains. Her death is what sparked the movement by those activist to send the others away. Three's okay for a herd, I guess, but two is not."

Emily brought up the information she had on the elephants in the wild. "Poachers are killing tens of thousands of Farwest elephants for their ivory tusk every year."

"Yeah, the Garlain don't have tusk. But still the criticism of keeping them in captivity has grown in recent years, we both know that," Deb said. "They've stopped trying to breed them. Mortality among baby elephants in zoos had gotten to three times what it is in the wild."

Emily nodded. "So most zoos have closed their exhibits and sent the animals to sanctuaries, and others have remodeled their enclosures to give their pachyderms more space."

Deb looked fondly at the picture up on the screen. "Yeah, I'd like to save the elephants."

"All right," Emily said, thoughtfully. "The elephants will be next."

Deb studied her friend and chuckled. "Next, for what?"

Emily met her gaze. She wanted so badly to be able to tell her about all the animals that they had helped thus far, but without showing her the Gnomes, she knew even Deb would have a really hard time believing her. To change the subject, she asked, "How long are you in town?"

Deb gave her a look of skepticism. "Since you look pretty much unscathed from your adventure, I could stay for a couple of days more to fill that need as a concerned friend. You know, keep an eye on you, and make sure you really are all right. But I have to be back at work on Monday."

"Cool. I'm going to take you to my next favorite place to hang out tomorrow. The Toft Aquarium. I know the head biologist there, he lets me go in the big tanks."

Deb raised a brow. "And what's in the big tanks?"

"Oh, a couple of baby whale sharks, and a giant manta."

"What!"

"I've been publishing a lot of papers on some of the endangered animals of Farwest Plains," Emily said, following the older woman outside. "I heard about your work with elephants and thought I'd look you up. I hope you don't mind all my questions."

"I've actually read some of your work," the woman said leading Emily to the courtyard where her hired hands were rounding up three baby elephants for their breakfast.

"Your article on the Pygmy Hippopotamus of Tehys Marsh was quite enjoyable."

"Thank you."

"How many others have you done?"

"A dozen or so. It keeps me busy and it pays the bills."

Emily took the bottle that the old woman handed her. Diane Sharrock was one of those heroines you never heard about on the news. She'd never have a school or street named after her, but she was a heroine just the same. In the span of her fifty years as a biologist, she had saved hundreds of orphaned elephants right there in her home in Rainobi.

Mrs. Sharrock and her late husband perfected the formula that simulates elephant milk, which proved to be crucial for those babies orphaned by poachers. Even though well into her 80's, she still got up every morning with the same dedication to keep these magnificent animals safe from extinction a bit longer.

Emily held the bottle tightly as the hungry little baby wrapped her trunk around it to guide it to her mouth to drink.

"We have three," Diane was saying. "The one you have is Rauja, our newest arrival. We believe she was born sometime in January 2015." The woman showed Emily some pictures of the baby that she carried in her apron pocket. "She was found in Gondwana, where we noted that a lot of animals are taking refuge these days. Besides the ivory trade, they have to deal with the destruction of their habitat. More farms are going up, more conflicts with local people. Not sure what happened to her mother. We have her labeled as Human / Wildlife Conflict. That's pretty much what we put on all of them these days."

"What will happen to her when she's old enough to be released?"

"She'll take her chances along with the others. Most stay around here in the preserve where they're safer."

Emily hugged and patted the young elephant. "Stay safe, little one." After saying goodbye to her host she walked back around to the side of the building, where she met up with the Gnomes.

Are we going to take the babies?" Masai asked.

Emily shook her head. "No, they'd die out in the wild, none of them have mothers."

"Where to?" Ptilopsis asked.

"Gondwana," Emily said, putting the images of the picture in her head.

"All elephants have several distinctive features," She whispered to the group of Gnomes as they watched the herd of giants from their hiding places in the tall grass. "The most notable, of course, is the long trunk. It has several purposes, particularly breathing, lifting water and grasping objects. Some elephants have tusk, which is just two incisors that have grown really long. They can be used as weapons and as tools for moving objects and digging. Elephants' large ear flaps help to control their body temperature. Their pillar-like legs can carry their great weight. They can weigh up to 15,000 pounds and stand around 13 feet tall. These are all females with their young, I'm guessing that one is the matriarch, because they seem to be following her lead. I don't see any bulls though," Emily said glancing down at Ptilopsis.

"Don't worry. Like the other animals we've saved, once we target a group, the rest will follow. We won't be leaving any wild ones behind."

Emily nodded and looked back at the elephants. The matriarch had her trunk up in the air and was starting to swing her front leg back and forth.

"Oh, no. I think the wind changed direction, she can smell us." Emily stayed hidden trying to remember what she had read about charging elephants. If ears are fanned they're going to charge, or is it if they're back flat...?

More of the herd started to show their displeasure of Emily's presence. There was a wall full of twitching trunks and swinging legs, mock charges, and of course, a chorus of trumpeting. Even the little ones would rush forward, only to run back to the safety of the adults.

Emily tried to slowly maneuver herself to get downwind again. Suddenly, the lead female started running right at her. Emily tried to get to her feet to run, but slipped, and grabbing the nearest thing which was Tegula she curled up into a little ball, sure that this was the end and she was going to be trampled or gored. She could feel the ground shaking with every step, and could tell the elephant was almost upon her. Then, as quickly as it had started, it stopped, and she could feel a gentle push on her cheek.

"You can get up now," Ptilopsis said.

Emily slowly opened her eyes to see the massive beast standing above her. Suddenly, there was a lot of activity as the rest of the herd crowded around them.

Trunks started probing her head, face, nose, and mouth. Instinctively she brushed them away as she tried sitting up.

"The Tall One has explained to her who you are," Ptilopsis said. "And what we are here to do."

Emily had let Tegula go, and watched as he too was being smothered with the herd's curious probing.

"Should we take them to Terra?" he asked, brushing away a trunk that seemed to be suctioned to the shell on his head.

"Yes," Emily said touching elephant and Gnome. "Let's take them to their new home."

Chapter Nine

Emily walked endlessly through the dense fog. After what seemed like hours, she finally came to a clearing in the mist. Before her stood the ruins of the Sacred Valley. The forest once again had overtaken the building, and like her first visit, it was still dark, wet and eerie to her. She moved hesitantly through the ruins, wondering why she was even there. She looked to the shrine where she had spotted the Northern White-faced Owl. In its place stood a beautiful woman whose blonde hair seemed to glow like the sun in this dank, darkened forest. Emily moved to within a couple of feet from her. Instinctively she knew who it was, and became overwhelmed with a feel of awe and wonder. "Cathleena?" she stammered.

The Goddess nodded.

"Why am I here?"

"You have questions and I want to give you the answers."

"I have no questions. I don't even believe in you."

"I'm real, come here and see for yourself."

Emily remained where she was and started to cry. "Why can't you be Ava, at least she's trying to help me. What have you ever done to help me?"

"Nothing. I destroyed the town you lived in and killed your family. I've done nothing to help you."

"What?" Emily said, in disbelief. "You! You caused the quake?"

"Yes, out of rage." Cathleena waved her hand, and the next thing Emily knew they were standing in the middle of a war-ravaged city. Bodies of people and animals alike littered the roads and door ways. Before Emily could comprehend what she was seeing, they were on the shores of a large body of water downstream from an oil refinery, surrounded by thousands of dead and decomposing fish. The scene changed again and they hovered on the dusty edge of a bleak and desolate strip mine where the ground had been torn away, and again the scene changed and they were now in a deforested area and witnessing a koala bear being electrocuted because it mistook an electric pole for a tree. Emily barely got her hand to her mouth when the scene once again changed and they were standing on a rocky beach looking at a carcass of an emaciated polar bear.

"You know why this beast died, do you not?"

"Global warming. No ice floes, no seals to hunt."

Before Cathleena could move them again, Emily turned on her. "Enough!" she yelled. "I know about the horrors of this world. I've been living them, remember?"

Emily tried to calm herself. "I get why you were mad. Man messed up. But why take it out on me?"

Cathleena shook her head sorrowfully. "I didn't target you."

The scene changed again and Emily was standing inside the goddess's old home.

"I was gone longer than I realized," Cathleena said, moving to the edge and looking out. "You've seen Terra." She glanced back, and seeing Emily nod, she continued. "That's pretty much how I had left Valencia. Great rainforest, woodlands, clean water, rolling prairies, lush green lands, mighty rivers, majestic mountain ranges. And now," she said with a sweep of her arm. "This is what I come back to."

Emily moved to the edge and looked down. Scenes like an old slide show played out in front of her. War, poaching, deforestation, strip mining, polluted waters, barren land, rivers dammed up, polar ice melting, poverty, sickness, and air pollution.

"I guess you messed up too, huh?" Emily said stepping back from the edge. "Maybe you shouldn't had left us on our own."

Cathleena turned, Emily thought for sure she saw a tear running down her cheek.

Moving to the center of the pavilion, she motioned Emily to join her. "It will take time, but I'm hoping to right my wrongs."

"What about Zorine? You weren't the only one in charge here."

Cathleena chuckled, "Believe me, you do not want her amongst us."

Cathleena closed her eyes, and a sense of calmness came over the marble structure. When she opened them again, she met Emily's stare, and said. "It's time for you to learn about your world."

"You should see all the classes I've taken, I know a lot about my world."

"This is not taught anymore in classrooms, I'm guessing it has not been for a long time," Cathleena said. Moving her hand, she created a small globe in the center of the pavilion. "My father created our world by using magic. Therefore, our world is magic, everything in it is magic. It surrounds us, and penetrates us, it binds us and our world together..."

Each rescue had its own unique challenges. Today they were in the Boretra Forest trying to convince man's closest known relative that their lives were in danger and that they needed to be moved. Emily looked up into the trees and watched as Masai was being tossed up and down by creatures that wanted to play more than they wanted to listen.

"What are these beast again?" Ptilopsis asked.

"Orangutans. They're in the great ape family. They were once widespread throughout the western foothills of the Reaches Mountains, from the Forest of Shadows all the way down to the Greater Woodlands. Now there's just this little patch of them here in the Boretra Forest."

"How did you like Cathleena?"

Emily gave the Gnome a sideways glance. "I guess I understand her better."

"It's a start. You may continue telling me about the Orangutans."

Emily chuckled. "Orangutans…They eat mostly fruit, they also eat some flowers, honey, bark, leaves and insects. They sleep in nests in the trees which they make every day from leaves and branches. They were put on the endangered species list because their habitats are being destroyed by deforestation."

"So you believe in her now?"

"What?"

"Cathleena, do you believe she exists now?"

"Well, I kinda have to. After all, I spent the whole day with her."

"Actually, you were gone five days, which reminds me, you're going to have to go to the store and get Zoe more food."

"Zoe has plenty of food. And was I really gone five days?"

"Yes you were, and Zoe is out of the food she likes."

"There's a whole case in the pantry. And it didn't seem like five days, the sun never went down, and I never got tired."

"She doesn't like that kind, she likes the stuff with the gravy. And in the heavens there is no night, nor the need to sleep."

"But the gravy is all she eats of that stuff, she wastes the chunks of meat because she doesn't eat it. Give her the pate, she'll eat it. And was I really in heaven? I thought you only go there when you die."

"She'll only eat it if she's starving. And this heaven is where the goddesses live, the underworld is where the dead go."

"Look, I'm not going to argue with you about Zoe's food. And you're really creeping me out. You mean everyone goes to hell when they die? I thought only the bad did."

"I told her I would ask you. And it's not hell, it's the underworld. Good or bad, that's where you go when you die."

"Well, tell her that the pate's all she's getting, so she'd better get used to it. And I'm done talking about the dead, let's change the subject."

"Fine, can we get back to the Orangutans?" Ptilopsis sighed.

"Yes," Emily said. "Where was I?"

"You were telling me why they were put on the endangered species list."

Emily tried collecting her thoughts. "Yes, their habitats are being destroyed by deforestation. Which is a big deal because they're totally arboreal, meaning they spend all their time in the trees. Even though they have a bulky body, they're very strong and, as you can see, quite agile. Look at their short bowed legs, their feet are like hands with an opposable big toe, and like humans, they have no tail." Emily sighed and looked thoughtfully from him to back up into the trees. "So how do we get them to Terra?"

"You could climb, but you should know by now that you have the power to put yourself anywhere you want to be," Ptilopsis said, touching her leg.

Cursing her lack of balance, Emily sat cautiously in an old nest that was probably built the day before. It didn't take long for Masai to talk the 2 year old juvenile that he'd been playing with into going and sitting with him and Emily in the nest. Once there, Emily took them to Terra. The air erupted into a flurry of sound and colors, birds, frogs, and insects were everywhere. She was stunned for a moment and thought maybe she had taken them to the wrong place.

Ptilopsis felt her concern and moved up beside her.

"I had no idea how many animals had been displaced by the deforestation," she said, moving down to the forest floor. "Looking around, she saw dozens of different types of parrots and toucans. There were lizards, too many to name, holler and spider monkeys, and there was even a sloth moving slowly along a branch above her head.

Ptilopsis stopped Emily's advance. Signaling her to remain quiet, he pointed to a form hidden in the underbrush.

Emily had to squat down to see under the lower branches. "Oh my, is that..." She studied it for moment longer, and then smiled at Ptilopsis. "It's a Boretra Jaguar. They're extinct on Valencia."

Emily paced back and forth by her map. "How many other animals are on Terra that have vanished from Valencia?"

Ptilopsis and Chelonia looked at each other and shrugged.

Emily sat in front of the little Gnomes standing on the desk. "What if we could bring them back? You know, repopulate the species we've lost."

"You're talking about the Jaguar?" Ptilopsis asked.

"Of course, I'm talking about the Jaguar."

"And put them where, Emily? In that little chunk of forest that we just took the Orangutan out of? This seems to mirror your argument about the orcas in captivity."

Emily looked at him angrily. "I'm going for a run," she said, storming off.

Ptilopsis got Tegula's attention. "Go with her, please?"

Tegula started to complain, then rushed off after her.

"I wish I had never shown her that beast," Ptilopsis said, after she left. "She's been obsessed with it since we got back."

"Maybe working on our next rescue will get her mind off of it," Chelonia suggested. "What animal did she mark?"

Both little Gnomes strained to see the map from where they were. Ptilopsis called to the smallest female. "What animal is next, do you know?"

Vulpes quickly jumped up onto the desk and turned on Emily's computer. Typing in a couple of key words, she brought up the list that Emily had made. The two older Gnomes looked on in awe.

"Vaquita," the small female said. "It's a porpoise. That's good because Emily likes being near the water."

Ptilopsis read aloud. "Vaquita, the world's most rare marine mammal, is on the edge of extinction. Vaquita are often caught and drowned in gillnets used within Panthalassa's Gulf of Filipe. More than half of the population has been lost in the last three years. It's estimated the Vaquita population at less than 60 now."

Vulpes looked at The Wise One with a look of alarm. "Only 60."

"We'll need to act quickly. Get everything ready for when Emily returns."

Emily walked out of the bedroom. As she was drying her hair, she looked over the information the Gnomes had laid out for her, then pushed it aside. "I was going to take these guys off the list."

"Why?" Tegula asked.

"Because I don't think we can help them anymore." She flipped the report his way and pointed to the date. "This is two years old. They're probably all dead now."

"We must try," Chelonia said.

"Yes, what if they're not all gone?" Sirenia added.

"Please Emily," Tegula said, touching her arm gently. "It wouldn't hurt to try."

Emily used a picture off the computer as a reference point and had the Gnomes take her to El Golfo de Santa Clara, Panthalassa. From there, she chartered a fishing boat owned by two brothers, Carlos and Nicolas, who agreed to take her out into the gulf so she could study the marine life.

"The Vaquita has a large dark ring around its eyes and dark patches on its lips," Nicolas said, as they stood by the stern. "Used to see them all the time out here."

"Have you seen any recently?"

He shook his head. "Not for a long time. Can't remember exactly when. Before the last winter solstice, I think."

The water in the gulf was around 80 degrees. Carlos handed Emily a mask and snorkel." The best way to see the marine life around here is getting in the water with them."

Emily unzipped her back pack and set it down next to the side of the boat so that when no one was looking, the Gnomes could climb out. Then, stripping down to her swimsuit, she donned the mask and snorkel and jumped off the side of the boat into the water with Nicolas.

The Gulf of Filipe was once known for its abundance of marine life, but over the past fifty years, the numbers of many species had declined. Nicolas pointed out a school of yellowtail followed closely by a couple of hammerhead sharks. She later found out that hammerheads used to swim in schools of up to a hundred individuals out there, but no more.

Swimming face down along the surface, looking at the animals below them, neither saw the mesh of danger directly ahead. Nicolas hit it first, catching his mask and then eventually his snorkel. Emily bounced off of it with her head, then realized what she had hit when glancing over at Nicolas. A discarded gill net that had been floating with the current was now draped over the young man's head and arm, and with all the struggling to free himself it was getting worse. Emily moved over to him in hopes of being able to set him free, but between them something else in the net caught her eye. A young Vaquita, stuck up to its dorsal fin in one of the holes of the net, was having a hard time surfacing to breathe. Emily looked from Nicolas to the trapped porpoise. Both were in dire need of rescuing, but which one to save first? Emily's mind raced as she swam to the entangled pair. Spitting out her mouth piece, she screamed for Tegula. She wrapped her arms around the porpoise while she extended her leg to touch Nicolas with her foot. Almost instantly, the two were free and the three floated for a moment in the water, looking at each other.

"Are you okay?" she asked.

Nicolas nodded, still a little surprised at his sudden freedom.

She grabbed his hand then said, "Good, let's get back to the boat."

It probably would have been better if Emily had put them back in the water, but the boat is what she pictured in her mind, and that's where Tegula placed them.

She and Nicolas landed heavily on the deck. Once she caught her breath from the impact, she laughed at the stunned look on both the brothers' faces. "I'm sorry, I can't explain. But thanks for taking me out to find the Vaquita. They'll be safe now."

With that, she pictured home as she felt a tiny hand touch her back.

Chapter Ten

It wasn't long after returning home that Emily started thinking about the jaguar again.

"Maybe we could bring some back and start a breeding program?" she suggested.

The six Gnomes lined the couch with array of mixed facial expressions. Finally Sirenia stood. "To bring an animal back that man has destroyed in the past is condemning it to die all over again. We can't do that."

Ptilopsis raised his hand. "I have a question?"

Emily sighed. "What is it?"

"Why are you so obsessed with this jaguar?"

"I saw one at the zoo when I was a kid."

"And?"

"And I can't believe they're all gone. I didn't take a picture of it, I barely noticed it. I feel like I should have done something." She sat in her chair, then finished. "I didn't even know that they went extinct until I was in college. That female that I saw in the zoo was one of the last."

"If you can fix the problems in your world, then someday we may be able to start bringing animals back, but until then..."

"They did it with the condor," Emily said, excitedly. "There were only 90 left, and they captured them and started captive breeding. A couple of years after that, they started releasing them back into the wild in areas where they wouldn't be affected by man. There's almost 600 of them now. I know we can fix the problems of our world."

"Unfortunately for some animals, there's not enough time," Ptilopsis said apologetically. "And I believe you still have the condor on your list of animals to be saved?"

Emily sighed. "Even though their numbers are on the rise, they're still considered endangered."

Ptilopsis patted her arm. "Who's next on the list?"

Emily sat down on a rock next to the Inner Sea, which is actually a really big lake in the mountains that separate the High Reaches from the Low Reaches. The lake was heavily used for boating and other water sports and was bustling with activity. The animal that she and the Gnomes were looking for was a tiny black tree frog which was found only in the high altitude lake, whose waters were naturally warmed by hydrothermal vents and stayed a pleasant 79 degrees all year long. Due to its small size, the tiny tree frog had numerous predators within its natural environment, including birds, rodents, lizards, toads and even larger frogs.

"This place has suffered great disturbances from human activities," Chelonia said sadly.

Emily gave a strained laugh. "Ah, yeah, you could say that."

"Are there fish in here?" Ptilopsis asked.

"Only what man stocks it with. There were a couple of different kind of native fish, I believe they were some kind of perch, but they all died out a long time ago. Now it's stocked with sport fish like bass and trout."

Tegula waded around the water in front of them, looking for movement by the banks.

"I don't think you'll find any of them in there," Emily said. "They'll be around the shoreline in the trees."

All six Gnomes looked at the shores of the lake. "There are no trees there."

Emily nodded. "Yep, that's the problem. They cut down most of the trees on the water's edge to put in dock, and to help keep debris out of the water so that boats wouldn't run into it."

"There's trees over there," Vulpes said, pointing to a row of five that someone had planted along their driveway. "Let's check over there."

"Too many people. I'll go over there. You guys check out that little patch of trees over there." Emily sent them to the eastern side, where a small group of ten trees surrounded a public camp site that didn't look to be in use at the moment.

Searching on hands and knees, Emily looked everywhere she could think of. There wasn't a lot known about these frogs, no one had ever seen a male, so whether it was larger or smaller than the female was unknown. She started looking under leaf litter and around ferns. A commotion off to her right distracted her from her work. A couple of children were playing around the swing set. Emily decided to go over and see if any of them had seen any of the tree frogs. When asked about the frog, a little boy pulled a jar out from under the porch of his trailer and showed it to Emily. Sure enough, it was a tiny black tree frog, but with no air holes in the jar's lid the little amphibian had already perished.

"Where did you find this at?" she asked.

"Down by the water."

"Can you show me where, please?"

"Sure."

Emily followed the little boy down to the water's edge. He pointed to a bushy plant, then turned around and went back to playing with his friends. Cursing the lack of Gnomes at that particular time, she slid down the bank and got into the water. Checking under leaves and debris, she found no adults, but did come across a small clutch of eggs on the underside of a leaf. Emily moved over to the area where she had sent the Gnomes. Her jeans were wet and starting to chafe her by the time she got to the campsite.

"What happened to you?" Tegula asked.

"I went wading."

"Oh."

Emily handed the eggs to him. "Can you tell if these are tree frog eggs?"

Tegula studied them, then handed them to Sirenia. The two Gnomes shook their heads. "They're not."

"Wait," a little voice said from behind her.

Emily froze where she was. Vulpes moved around her, touching her leg. "Take us to Terra."

Emily did as she was instructed. When they arrived, Vulpes took the small frog off Emily's back and placed it near the lake shore.

"There's another one off the list," Vulpes said.

"Well, it's a good thing she found me, because I wasn't having much luck locating her." Emily looked across the Inner Sea of Terra and sighed. It was so peaceful and quiet. Glancing to her right, she could see dozens of tiny black frogs on the tree next to her.

"This place is so different from Valencia, it's hard to believe that except for man, they were made identical."

Emily and the Gnomes made their way down to the water's edge and sat for hours by the clear, tranquil lake, forever free from any kind of disturbance from man.

For the next year and a half, Emily traveled all around the world, to find and rescue the endangered spices of Valencia. Animals like the South Range penguin, the wild dog, the armadillo of Panthalassa, the camel, the brown bear, the fishing cat, the mongoose of the Garlain Plains, the lower Maygar River dolphin, the Tehys Marsh gharial, and the pygmy hippopotamus. The Greater Woodlands red panda, the chimpanzee, and the tortoise. She covered land and sea to reach every precious creature, including the fin and the mighty blue whale that swam in the Pangaea Ocean. And so, so many more. She work hard, really hard, to save them all.

And then the day came. Looking out into the west, she watched as Northern Straits orcas frolicked in the setting sun. They were to be the last to go to Terra, and she was going to miss them very much. To her surprise, there had already been some reports about the missing animals. Of course, the people that missed them were the ones that used to exploit them, but most people didn't seem to even care that they were gone. This saddened Emily deeply. Moving away from the lighthouse, she climbed down to water's edge where Tegula and his friends were waiting. Emily took a picture of her beloved whales, then knelt down and laid her hand on Nanna's head and bid her farewell. A hand gently rested on her shoulder and the scene seem to skip a frame, but then it was back to normal again. The only difference was that there was no lighthouse on the cliff above them. Emily wrapped her arms around her drawn up knees.

"Stay?" Vulpes said, nudging closer to her.

"Yes, please stay?" Masai added.

Emily touched both of them gently on the cheek.

"Yes, Emily you must stay," Sirenia said, with a saddened face. "Who will take care of the animals if you don't stay?"

"You will," she said giving her a hug. "And besides, who will take care of the animals that we left back on Valencia if I don't return?"

Chelonia hung his head and gave Emily's leg a gentle pat. Then Ptilopsis moved by her side as well and laid his hand on her arm.

"You don't want me to send Zoe your way, do you?"

Ptilopsis thought for a moment then nodded. "Fancy Feast is not obtainable out here, but I believe she could adjust. Yes, I would like her company, but wouldn't you miss her?"

"I'm away from home so much, it's not really fair to her. Besides, I can always come visit, right?"

Ptilopsis disappeared for a second, then reappeared with Zoe beside him. "She has agreed," he said, scratching her chin.

Emily was starting to get even more blurry eyed as she said goodbye to her cat, but even through the haze of her tears she could tell the area in front of her grew brighter in intensity. And once she was able to see again, she saw the two goddesses down by the water's edge. Cathleena moved above the water, happily greeting each of her whales.

Ava turned to Emily, "You have done well. And let it be known that if you ever possess the desire to come back, you are welcome here."

Emily wiped her nose on her sleeve. "There's still a lot to be done on Valencia," she said, drying her tears. "Somehow, I've got to get mankind to stop destroying the planet and hurting the animals, before I'm forced to send them all here."

"Yes, there is a lot to do," Cathleena said, floating up the bank. "But you will not be alone in your crusade. I have petitioned my father to allow me to govern over

Valencia again. Also, The Young One wishes to remain with you, Ava and I see no reason why he cannot. With him, you will always be able to tap into the magic of these two worlds."

Emotions overtook her, and not caring if it would be proper or not, Emily rushed into Cathleena's arms and gave her a hug. Surprisingly, the embrace was returned. Feeling Tegula's hand on her leg, Emily thought of home.

The End

Made in the USA
San Bernardino, CA
29 May 2017